The
EASTER MAN

Reviews for
THE DUTTON GIRL

**A novel and the first book
in this series of
John Nolan stories**

**Published by
Coffeetown Press of Seattle
in June of 2018**

"Deftly entertaining . . . Certain to be an immediate and popular addition to both the personal reading list of dedicated mystery buffs and community library mystery/suspense collections."
THE MIDWEST BOOK REVIEW

"A classic whodunit . . . The author does a fantastic job at intertwining historical facts through this story . . . Progresses at a steady pace, giving just the right amount of clues and action to keep you entertained . . . Interesting and believable."
READER VIEWS

"(John Nolan has) the quiet, self-possessed demeanor of a star detective with an understated talent for his craft and an appealing habit for being right when others are wrong. His slow, methodical investigation is fun to witness . . . Competently crafted, with a bevy of suspicious characters and a pleasing variety of bum leads . . . However, the most compelling aspect of the book is not who took a spoiled heiress or even Nolan himself, but, rather, how rich, poor, and working-class New Yorkers lived and interacted in the World War I era."
MANHATTAN BOOK REVIEW

Reviews for

FIRE IN THE RECTORY

and two more John Nolan detective novellas

Published in March of 2019

★★★★★ – *5 out of 5 stars*

"Excellent ... Each tale has twists and turns I could never manage to predict. Was the fire an accident or arson? Is Mr. Hughes truly the sort of man he seems? If the most obvious suspect did indeed commit the murder, where is his weapon? I didn't even try to guess the answers to these questions but merely let the story take me along for the ride."

MANHATTAN BOOK REVIEW

"Engrossing ... One of Fire in the Rectory's strengths lies in its historical accuracy, which brings the era and its culture to life ... All the stories excel in a fine balance of whodunit, politics, cultural inspection, and a sense of 1900s America."

THE MIDWEST BOOK REVIEW

"Ingenious writing ... Set during the time of World War I when immigrants were arriving in force to the United States, the author shows how bigotry, poverty, and corruption prevailed with his well-researched historical facts."

READER VIEWS

The EASTER MAN

A John Nolan detective novel

by

STAN FREEMAN

HAMPSHIRE HOUSE PUBLISHING CO.
FLORENCE, MASS.

THE EASTER MAN

by Stan Freeman

Hampshire House Publishing Co.

www.hampshirehousepub.com

© 2020 by Stan Freeman

All photo illustrations are by the author.

Manufactured in the United States of America

ISBN: 978-1-7344384-3-7

JOHN NOLAN   *SHEENAGH NOLAN*

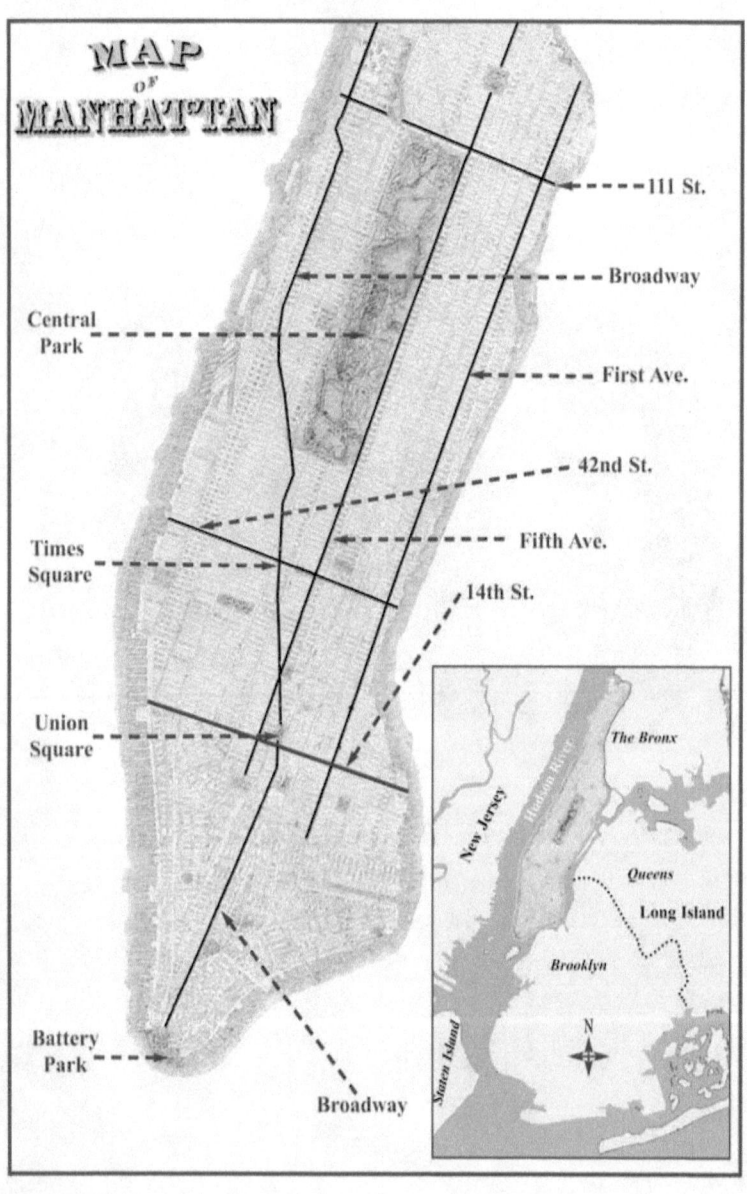

Peter Schwegel by the River Clyde

1

Watch on the River

A FEROCIOUS GALE blew across the central regions of the British Isles on January eighteenth, 1916, forcing many ships bound for Dublin and Liverpool to move north into the River Clyde in Scotland for shelter.

In Glasgow, a man had been standing on the cobblestones of the quayside on the river's north bank much of the cold, dreary morning, watching the procession of steamers, schooners, clippers, and other ships in the channel. He had counted three military ships, including a British armored cruiser.

Now he was joined by an older man – stout, a scruffy gray beard, perhaps sixty – who handed him an envelope. "It's done. In my opinion, it's very good work."

The younger man, whose passport it would be, drew out the document and examined it.

NAME: Robert James McFee
AGE: 28
PROFESSION: Chemist

PLACE AND DATE OF BIRTH:
        Bishopbriggs, Scotland, Jan. 13, 1888
HEIGHT: 5 feet 8 inches
Forehead: High
Eyes: Brown
Hair colour: Light brown
Complexion: Fair
Any special peculiarities: Scar under chin

The photograph, shot with a magnesium flash lamp in a basement at midnight, was, to his eye, sufficient. At least he was recognizable.

Also tucked into the envelope was a first-class steamer ticket. *The Bristol Star*. Glasgow, Scotland, to Halifax, Canada. Departing from Prince's Dock on February twenty-sixth. Arriving Halifax on March eighth.

"What do you think?" the older man asked. "Is the passport good enough?"

"I'm not the one to say. Why don't you take it down to those customs men and ask them."

"How would that go, then?" the older man mused. "Good sirs, if you don't mind, will these papers get my German friend here onto your steamship?"

"I'm not German."

"Austrian. No difference. We're on the same side in this business."

Both men spoke perfect English tinged with Scottish accents, as both were educated in Scotland. Schwegel – McFee's real name was Peter Schwegel – was a chemist, a specialist in explosives. He was born in Austria, where his late mother was from, but his father, still alive, was Scottish.

The older man was a German operative in Scotland

and a specialist in helping agents reach America.

War was raging in Europe, and while America still had not entered the conflict, declaring itself neutral, it was shipping vast amounts of munitions and other supplies to England and its allies. In effect, it had become a combatant in the eyes of Germans, drawing the attention of German agents.

Schwegel, who began with Abteilung IIIb, the German military intelligence division, gathering intelligence in Scotland, had only recently been recruited for overseas espionage. This was to be his first assignment.

A ferry venturing out into the crowded channel from the York Street landing passed too close to the bow of a steamer, bringing a blast from the larger ship's horn.

"Speaking of customs," the older man said as he buttoned his overcoat. "In New York, how do you plan to get your bombs into the cargo of the freighters?"

"I don't. Watch these ships here being loaded. Yes, they check what goes on board very carefully. But they don't spend any time checking the exteriors, the hulls. I don't imagine they do in New York either."

"So you'll attach them to the hulls?"

"Yes, below the water line. They'll all be timed to go off within minutes of each other on Easter Sunday."

"When is Easter?'

"April twenty-third. Less than three months away."

"And how many bombs are you talking about?"

"Let me just say … many. We'll not only bomb ships in the harbor, but also buildings and private homes in Manhattan. The Americans will be warned. We can get to you. Stay out of the war. It will be a day they'll remember."

"How you do it is your business, not mine, I suppose.

In fact, it's better that I don't know. As they say, don't let the left hand know what the right is doing."

"*Lass die rechte Hand nicht wissen, was die Linke tut.*"

The older man smiled. "It's strange. I never speak German while I'm in Glasgow. A personal rule. But when I hear German, I feel a thrill at the words. I also feel a longing to be home, and, to be honest, a desire to not be doing this."

Schwegel turned. "Why? It's exciting, isn't it? War is tremendously exciting."

"You're too young, McFee." He paused a moment as they both watched the slow dance of ships in the channel. "I suppose it's because I like the Scottish people, and I find I can't look my Scottish friends in the eye, men I've known for two decades. I feel, well, I feel a bit dirty by doing what I'm doing. Sometimes I wish I were in the trenches doing the work of a gentleman." The older man turned to Schwegel. "You don't have that problem?"

"I believe completely in what I'm doing. And the Americans – I have no feeling for them at all. They are idiots, *blödsinnig*. This day of explosions will serve them right for shipping arms to our enemies."

The older man slowly shook his head. "All aren't idiots. It's a mistake to think you can sum up the Americans in a single word and that's all they are. I don't mean offense, but that's lazy thinking."

Schwegel smirked.

The older man took hold of his arm and squeezed it. "A warning, my friend. If you're going to be working in America, it'd be, my God, a terrible mistake, the very worst mistake you could make, to underrate them."

John Nolan at work on Broad Street

2

The Accountant

THAT SAME DAY, New York City was enduring some of the coldest weather of the winter, with temperatures near zero as the city awoke.

In Brooklyn, a court magistrate had to suspend arraigning prisoners when the ink froze on his desk. On lower Broadway at Spring Street, several of the horses still at work in the city hauling freight slipped and fell on the ice. People distressed by the animals' suffering brought more than a dozen blankets out of stores and apartments to spread across the intersection.

Nevertheless, when lunchtime arrived in the financial district at the lower end of Manhattan, the vast army of workers, of tellers and typists, of accountants and actuaries, poured out of towering office buildings and onto the icy sidewalks to locate their noon meal, often purchased from curbside vendors' carts.

John Nolan, an accountant with the Demers & Demers investment firm on Broad Street, would have been one more anonymous soldier in this army, except that he was still enjoying the notoriety − at least in his office − brought on by an article two days earlier in the *Evening Telegram*.

It was about the rough-and-tumble life of private detectives and the toll the profession takes on those who practice it.

A year ago, John Nolan was just twenty-seven but already one of the most highly regarded detectives in the city. However, he was about to be married and hoping to reduce the dangers presented by his profession, he obtained his accounting certificate and began working a part-time side job as a bookkeeper on Broad Street.

Two weeks ago, though, facing the responsibilities of impending fatherhood, he turned to the columns and numbers full-time at the behest of his wife.

"As a detective, I'd estimate that once a month, something happens to put you in peril, and that's too often for my taste," said Mr. Nolan, who made his name by solving the notorious Dutton kidnapping case after the city police failed in their attempt.

Nolan bought a tin of fish soup and salted crackers from a street vendor then slowly navigated through the sidewalk crowds back to his office.

On his first day at Demers & Demers, he was proudly told that their modern, seventeen-story building, home to the International Paper Company and other large corporations, stood on land that that had been home to a barracks of the Continental Army during the Revolution. ("If those boys could only see what it's all become!" one of the Demers told him.) Fighting the jostling crowds every day at noon was one of the things that made him wonder what, indeed, they would think.

Two women smiled at him as he passed on the sidewalk. With his black hair and fine features, he would have drawn the attentions of women for no other reasons than that. However, there was something in his eyes, a look of well-earned self-reliance, that made him that much more attractive to them in such an intimidating city.

He was approaching the front entry when he saw Sean Tierney come out of the lobby. Their eyes met.

"Cousin, I been looking for you," Tierney said. "Can we talk? I have a job that's come up."

"I'm not coming back, Sean."

"I'm not asking you to exactly. But let's move inside, why don't we."

Big and burly, standing well over six feet, Tierney was a former New York City policeman who had been advised to resign in 1913. A corruption scandal had unfolded in his precinct involving protection money paid to foot patrolmen by local hotels catering to prostitutes. So he founded a detective agency and hired Nolan, a fresh arrival from Ireland. However, he paid his smaller, younger cousin – Nolan was five feet nine and had a lean athleticism – only fourteen dollars a week. ("That's what everyone pays Irish right off the gangplank, but the fact you're my cousin got you an extra dollar.")

For the year Nolan worked for him, trying to earn enough to bring his fiancée over from Ireland, Tierney never raised the wages once, even after Nolan's success with the Dutton kidnapping. And when Demers & Demers beckoned, offering him nearly twice the money, he did not hesitate to quit.

The lobby of Nolan's building was nearly as cold as the street since the doors were constantly opening for employees returning from lunch. The two men moved to a back wall away from the elevators and the flow of people. The steam from Nolan's soup and their collective breath fogged the air between them.

"All right, Sean. What do you want? And hurry up. I want to eat this before it freezes."

"I'm not asking you to return, except just for one job that's more accounting than anything. It's not dangerous in the least."

"I'm not a detective anymore, Sean. Sheenagh is due in five months."

"This is just a few hours and that's all. And I'll pay a lot." Nolan shook his head.

"Cousin, don't you even want to know what it is?"

"All right. What is it?"

"Go ahead, sip your soup, why don't you. A man what's a partner in a printing company over on Hudson Street, Cabot and Schulz, he thinks his partner is embezzling from him. He don't know anything about the fine details of accounting books, though, and I don't knows anything either, but you do."

"Which is Cabot and which is Schulz."

"One is one and the other is the other. What do you care?"

"Which is the embezzler?"

"Oh. That'd be Schulz," Tierney said.

"Cabot sounds English. What's Schulz?"

"Sounds German to me."

"They're fighting their own little European war, I guess," Nolan said.

"Yeah. So what I'm asking," Tierney said, growing impatient, "is if you can take a few hours this Sunday morning, when Schulz is out of town, to come down to the printing business with me and see what you can find in the ledgers."

"Sunday?"

"That's when the embezzler is gone, yeah. You can honestly tell Sheenagh it's only an accounting job."

"Sunday is church, Sean."

"Sunday is still church, is it? Well, I didn't know that," Tierney leaned in, towering over Nolan. "Look, cousin. I'll pay you twenty dollars for the day. Twenty dollars is still worth something to the highly paid accountants of the world, ain't it?"

Nolan sipped his soup and thought. Yes, it was worth something. It was worth quite a lot when you're only making twenty-five dollars a week.

He sighed with resignation. "What time Sunday?"

Strikers on Hudson Street

3

The Bookkeeping Scheme

NOLAN TOOK THE elevated to Manhattan then a trolley to Hudson Street. At nine o'clock on a Sunday morning, there were barely any riders on the streetcar, just a family with young children sitting across the aisle. The parents were whispering back and forth and Nolan wondered why until he heard the German words *guten* and *essen* – good and eat.

Anti-German feeling in America was growing and many German-Americans were becoming fearful of showing any signs of German heritage. After the steamer *Lusitania* was sunk by a German U-boat in May 1915, killing 1,198, including 128 Americans, the open hostility against German-Americans became widespread and blatant.

Weeks earlier, Nolan had gone into a toy shop in Brooklyn with Sheenagh so she could buy a rattle. Above the register was a sign. "We have German toy soldiers if your boy needs Germans for his soldiers to kill."

However, riding the trolley now, he could sympathize with a simple immigrant family – German or not – trying to survive in New York. After all, his was one of them.

Getting off at Hudson and Spring streets on the city's West Side, he saw a crowd of men on the sidewalk up ahead. As he walked toward them, curious more than anything, Tierney ran up to him from behind and grabbed his shoulder.

"Don't go no further, Nolan," he said. "They're strikers."

"What does that have to do with where we're going?"

"Cuz it's the photoengravers at Cabot and Schulz what's on strike, and there's strikebreakers inside what's running the presses. That bastard Cabot didn't tell me about this."

Nolan stopped and looked at the mob. He knew the character of strikers in New York. Many would be carrying pistols or knives. "If we go in, we'll be jumped coming out," he said.

"Let me think." Tierney assessed the situation. The frigid weather had broken over the city and temperatures, while still chilly, were at least tolerable.

"All right. I'll get Cabot to pay you ten dollars more out of his pocket. But you're going in without me. No sense both of us in there."

"Then I want your twenty right now. Sheenagh wouldn't let me come unless I can put it in her hands the moment I get back. She doesn't want me doing detective work anymore."

"I don't have it with me, cousin."

"I know you have that folded twenty hidden in your wallet."

Tierney frowned and got it. "So Sheenagh gave you her permission to come, did she." He slapped the bill into Nolan's hand.

"Wait 'til you're married someday. You'll see how it is."

Within a few minutes, Cabot turned the corner, a small dapper man wearing a black winter coat with a fur collar and cuffs.

"Mr. Cabot, sir," Tierney said. "Maybe I missed it, but I don't think you told me about a strike."

"We'll be able to get in. I have my men out front with shotguns – see them by the truck bay? – but four uniformed policemen will be joining us at any moment to accompany us inside."

"What about coming out," Nolan asked. "When I leave, are the police going to walk me out?"

"Unfortunately, I only have them for a half hour. So, I'm afraid —"

Nolan began to walk away down Hudson Street.

"Wait, Nolan." Tierney grabbed his arm, then turned to Cabot. "Mr. Cabot, sir, this detective, who is also a certified accountant and just the man you need for this, he has to be convinced it's worth putting his well-being in jeopardy to do this job. What can you pay him extra, right out of your pocket right now, to convince him?"

Cabot thought a moment. "I think I might be able to add five dollars."

"Fifteen," Nolan said with cold directness.

Cabot smiled at the young man's shrewdness then reluctantly took out the bills.

"And I want your armed guards to walk me to the trolley after this is over," Nolan said. "One more thing, Sean.

I need your revolver. I'll return it in a couple of days."

"I didn't bring it."

Nolan flung back Tierney's coat lapel to reveal the holstered Smith & Wesson on his shoulder.

"I guess I forgot I was wearing it."

—◦—⬥—◦—

The four police officers, with Nolan and Cabot at their center, walked toward the building. The unruly strikers swore at them and waved table legs and mop handles but allowed them through.

The printing shop took up all the first and second floors. Various machines – presses, folders, trimmers, binders, stampers, and coaters – were going full throttle so that Nolan could not hear a word Cabot was saying as they crossed the work floor of the main room.

In Cabot's office, even with the door closed, it was not much easier to hear him.

"The next office, that door there, that's Schulz's. The ledgers are all in there. I'm guessing you know what to look for. I'll be out on the floor, if you need anything."

Within an hour, Nolan found a crack in the wall of Schulz's scheme. A half hour later, it had all fallen. He located Cabot supervising the loading of a delivery truck.

"You figured it out? My God, that was fast."

Back in Cabot's office, Nolan had laid out the evidence on the man's desk.

"You have contractors for some jobs, isn't that right?" Nolan asked.

"We don't do three-color printing, only black and white and two-color. So yes, we hire contractors for three-color."

"Two years ago, I'm guessing, your Mr. Schulz began

requiring these contractors to send in their invoices on his form, not theirs. See, here's one on his form."

"I remember. He said it made it easier for our girls to figure out what the charges were for, if all the invoices were identical."

"Well, your Mr. Schulz took his blank forms – here's one of them – and wrote invoices himself for jobs no one did and then mixed them in with the real invoices, figuring no one would ever notice. I tried to match all the invoices with jobs you got bids on. I found this stack of seven invoices here, all from the same company, Mueller Printing, with no bids and no proof in your records that any work was ever done. And the handwriting is the same on all of them."

"Let's see ... My God. That's Schulz's hand for certain." He shook his head in disbelief as he examined the invoices. "How much do they add up to?"

"Over two years, about $8,600."

"Oh my God. So he wrote checks to himself?"

"No. He wrote them to Mueller Printing, but I'll bet if you go down to the city and check the records, you'll find the company is registered in his name. I can't find any Mueller Printing in the industry directories you have. Now, look here. This is Schulz's personal check ledger, which was right on top in his desk drawer. There's a man he wrote seven personal checks to around the same time as each invoice, and they add up to nearly $8,600. See right here?"

"Frederick Kohler. I don't recognize the name. How do we find out who he is?"

Nolan and Cabot gazed at each other for a moment as they both thought about it.

Then Nolan smiled. "Well, there's one way."

He picked up the earpiece on Schulz's desk telephone, leaned toward the mouthpiece, then pushed on the holder several times.

"Central ... Do you have a number for a Frederick Kohler ... Ends in CK, then K ... O ... H ... Yes, Kohler ... You do? Can you connect, please?"

Nolan tipped the earpiece toward Cabot so they could both listen.

Someone picked up. "Hello?"

"Yes, is this Frederick Kohler?"

"Let me guess. You want to know if the rally tomorrow is changed because of the weather. Well, it is. You got a pen?"

"Uh, yes sir."

"We're moving inside to the German Club at a hundred and twelve, West 59th. Starting at the same time, though, at six. You want to know what time I'm speaking? That's been changed too."

"Please."

"I'm moved to first on the bill, at six fifteen."

"Can I ask your topic?"

"The topic is just what you think it is. Keeping America out of the war. Stopping America from sending munitions to England. Didn't you guess that's my topic?"

"Uh, yes sir."

"Well, I hope we'll see you there." Then he hung up.

Aberdeen, Scotland

4

Home to Aberdeen

ON JANUARY TWENTY-THIRD. a month before the *Bristol Star* was to sail, Schwegel took the train to Aberdeen for a visit home.

On Scotland's eastern coast, a hundred and fifty miles from Glasgow, Aberdeen was an ancient city − it had been settled for nearly eight thousand years. It was also a city that sparkled. Literally sparkled. Many of its churches, schools, and municipal buildings were constructed with locally quarried granite that had a high content of mica. So in the sunlight, the flecks of mica flashed as if they were diamonds.

Schwegel had not been home in nearly a year. His mother was dead, taken in his youth by consumption, and his father, who was fifty-one when his son was born, retired early from the University of Aberdeen, where he taught botany, because of chronic lung disease. Now his father was drawing closer to death. His hearing nearly gone, he sat much of the day in the sunroom of his tiny stone cottage on Queens Road, trying to read scholarly journals, smoking a pipe, and staring out the window.

His father refused to get a telephone and had answered neither of the letters his son had written him since Christmas. And he had become increasingly belligerent about minor things toward the students who were hired to cook and clean for him.

Arriving home on a day of near record warmth for late January, Schwegel found the front door unlocked.

"Father? Anyone home?"

Getting no response, he set his valise on the stairs and walked through the house. He finally saw him in the backyard garden, dozing on a sun chair, a straw hat covering his bald head, a lap blanket around his shoulders, drool on his chin. To his son, he looked so pitiful, so ridiculous. Would he not be better off dead? Living alone and now his faculties going – what was left?

Upstairs, Schwegel found his small bedroom was rapidly becoming a storage room, crowded to the point of being unrecognizable with unwanted clothes, discarded furniture, and stacks of newspapers.

Following his parents divorce when he was four, he moved back to Austria from Scotland with his mother. She died when he was nine, devastating him, and he was shipped back to Aberdeen and his father.

Schwegel cleared space on the bed, propped the pillow against the headboard, and stretched out. Remnants of his childhood could be seen on the walls and beneath the clutter. A first ribbon in science, another in biology, various framed diplomas and scholarly citations.

Here, there was no Robert McFee. There was only Peter Schwegel, the friendless nine-year-old, spending the afternoons doing his schoolwork, shooting an air rifle at squirrels from the window, examining female anatomy in the colored plates in his father's medical books, smoking cornsilk cigarettes.

In school in Aberdeen, his initial lack of fluency in English made him the foreigner, the stranger, to children his age. And that stuck with him, creating a theme in his early life in Scotland. The outsider. How he resented it.

He spent summer vacations in Austria with his cousins, only reinforcing the sense that he was Austrian and not Scottish or British.

After graduation from Aberdeen's high school, he went on to study chemistry at Mason Science College in Birmingham, England, then he took a position in an industrial chemicals company on the outskirts of London after graduating. However, his Scottish-English with a tinge of a German accent sounded to many native Englishmen like a foreign language, again casting him as the outsider both in college and in London, which only added to his resentment. So when war was declared, a schism that had existed in him for two decades suddenly had an expression in life. He found he instantly sided with Austria and Germany against Scotland and England. Let this be a lesson to them. Ostracize him and pay for it.

He was visiting relatives in Austria at the outbreak of the conflict in July 1914. The following day, he went in to the local military office to volunteer. Learning his background, especially his fluency in English, the recruitment officer referred him to the Abteilung IIIb, the espionage service. He was sent back to Scotland through the Netherlands, which was steadfastly neutral, to work as an intelligence agent.

Now he looked around his bedroom. Between two stacks of newspapers, he spotted his old bookshelf and his worn copy of *Treasure Island*. His heart jumped at the sight of the crimson red cover. He first read it in the summer of 1896 when he was eight and living in Austria. It was still his favorite novel.

He went over, drew it off the shelf, and turned the yellowing pages. Billy Bones, Jim Hawkins, Dr. Livesey, Long John Silver. Reading the names, he had to smile.

As he turned more pages, though, it was as if his heart slowly realized it was no longer allowed to feel such affection, such fondness, toward anything – and the thrill of discovering it on the shelf began to vanish. He closed it and stared at the cover, at the gold lettering and red fabric, feeling betrayed by this book, by the joy that it and so much of his early youth in Austria promised but failed to deliver. Instead, the naive happiness he felt in 1896 had given way to the icy stillness, the subtle cruelty, he felt in 1916.

Indeed, he did not want to feel as he did in 1896. Such feelings were weak, feeble, *schwach*. He had to admit that with the adventure of the war, he felt a thrill at living in 1916. 1916 was about strength, power, *stärke*.

—◆—

"What are you doing now? Are you working?" his father asked in his precise Scottish accent.

They were eating from trays in the sunroom. Leftover veal, leftover potatoes, steamed greens.

"In Glasgow, at a chemical company." Abteilung IIIb had only recently given him the forged papers for his work identity. Sales agent for Deecks & Co.

"Speak up."

"A chemical company in Glasgow."

"What's its name?"

"Deecks and Company."

"Say again?"

"Deecks. It's a chemical company."

"Never heard of it. Are you doing war work?'

"Some. In fact, I may have to travel to Canada for several months. I might not be home until after the summer."

A lengthy silence followed.

"What about Anja?" His father asked. "She's still in England. Have you seen her lately?"

"Not in a while."

"You should write her. She's your cousin."

"I will when I get back."

In fact, he had no intention of ever contacting her again. He had not seen her in six years, since his last term at Mason Science College in Birmingham. Fourteen years older than him and his first cousin, she was also living in Birmingham, working as a nurse in the city prison, while he was at the college. He had taken her to dinner a half dozen times, gradually feeling a warmth toward her that he had not felt for any other woman. However, when he confessed his love for her, she rejected him in a callous fashion.

"Oh, Peter, you're much too studious. I would find that life terribly boring. I need excitement and I just wouldn't find it with you."

That comment still infuriated him.

"What about a wife?" His father asked. "Do you have a wife yet?"

"I don't want a wife."

"Every man wants a wife."

"I'm not every man."

His father turned toward him. "Get a wife for God's sake, Peter."

Momentarily, they fell back into silence. Finished with his meal, Schwegel wondered if it might create the opportunity for him to leave the room gracefully.

"You know you're going to be conscripted soon," his father said. "They passed the act and it takes effect in the next few months. You say you're supposed to go to Canada. You might not want to leave Scotland just yet."

"My business is considered military so I'll be deferred. I'm not worrying."

"Worrying? I would think you'd want to be in the thick of this instead of selling … what did you say it was?"

"Chemical explosives."

His father went back to picking at his veal and the conversation stopped. Schwegel knew his father supported the Allies. So he never mentioned his own sympathies to him. In fact, his father believed he fully supported the Allied cause.

After dinner, his father dozed on the sofa, eventually lying down and pulling a lap blanket over himself. A nightly habit, his son guessed.

Schwegel poured a glass of brandy and studied his father. Motionless, his eyes closed, he looked no different than he would in death. So eerie.

As Schwegel rose to go up to his room, he accidentally kicked a chair leg and his father opened his eyes, apparently not fully asleep.

"I'm going to talk to Dean Campbell tomorrow," his father said. "He heads the Aberdeen board that advises on personal deferments. Do you want me to ask him to see if he can stop yours?"

"Why would I want that?"

"Don't you want to be in this war? Don't you want to do your part for your country?"

"I am in it. My company is in it. They do important work."

"That's not you, though. It's your company. With your knowledge of German, don't you think you could be more useful?"

"I'm being useful already."

"No you're not. Peter, I think you're avoiding this war. If you are, I don't admire you for it."

"I can't help what you admire and don't admire and I don't care."

"You don't want to be called a coward, do you?"

Provoked, Schwegel started to say something more to defend himself. Perhaps he would tell him the truth, but knowing his father, knowing his thick-headed ideas of patriotism, he would likely turn his own son in to Scottish authorities.

No, just let the old fool die, Schwegel thought as he turned to leave. In fact, he would welcome the news. Please, old man, just do me a favor and die.

Scheenagh Nolan

5

Shopping for the Baby

A S SCHWEGEL WALKED out of his sunroom in
Aberdeen, Nolan stood in his front room in
Brooklyn just after lunch, trying again to reach his cousin
on the telephone, the only private phone in his building,
to tell him what had happened at Cabot and Schulz.

After four bells and no answer, he hung up.

"John, what are we going to be able to spend?"
Sheenagh called from the bedroom where she was dressing.

The Professional Women's League was to begin a
three-day charity bazaar in an hour, featuring infant
clothes and furnishings, in the Thirteenth Regiment
Armory in Brooklyn. A week earlier, Sheenagh made
him promise to take her for the opening day, when the
choices were best, even though the baby was not due
until June.

Nolan drew out his household budget ledger. They
lived in a ground-floor, four-room apartment in a tenement on Clinton Avenue in Brooklyn. Rent was thirty

dollars a month and food was nearly as much, so most of the few dollars extra in his paycheck each week went into a savings account, which at the moment held two hundred forty-three dollars.

"Did Sean pay you for this morning?" Sheenagh shouted from the bedroom.

"He did."

"Can we use that money for the bazaar?"

"I suppose we can." He did not tell her about the fifteen dollars Cabot had given him.

"And you're done, right? Dat was your last detective job?"

"*That*, dear, not *dat*. Yes, it was the last one."

They were both struggling to soften their Irish accents as much as possible, even taking an evening class once a month at Erasmus High School, *American Speech*. Their assignment this month was to learn to pronounce the "h" in any "th" word. So "tink" would become "think" and "dis" would become "this."

They had largely succeeded with the previous month's assignment, turning their "i's" from the Irish "oy" to the American "eye." So "Oil be going" finally became "I'll be going."

Now Sheenagh walked into the front room and twirled about in a white linen dress she had sewn based on newspaper illustrations.

"How do I look? Does it show?"

He had to smile. They had known each other since childhood. Nearly two decades later, he could still feel a thrill looking at her sweet face and figure. "Lovely," he said.

"But do I show?"

"Don't you want to? I would think at a baby bazaar, it

would be a badge of honor."

"You either want to show a lot or not at all. If it's a lit-tle, you just look fat. No one can tell it's a baby. Hand me my coat and let's go."

—◆—≫—◆—

Nolan first saw Sheenagh in 1896 as she timidly entered his grammar school classroom in rural Tinryland, Ireland, southwest of Dublin, at the start of the school term. Serving all grades, boys and girls, in one room, the school was run by the Sisters of the Sacred Heart.

She was five. He was nine. To him, she resembled his sisters' dolls. Perfectly almond-shaped eyes and heart-shaped face. It was his earliest memory of finding a girl's face beautiful.

Nolan could vividly recall a moment that first day. He was sitting two rows away from her but even with her in their rows. The nun leading the discussion of trees told the class to look out the side window at a goat willow that had lost one of its multiple stems in an overnight windstorm. Instead, Nolan glanced sideways at this striking new girl to find that she was staring at him. She smiled. His heart raced. After that, he never lost the sense of a shared destiny with her.

In 1898, when Nolan was eleven-years-old, his great uncle, John Murphy, more than sixty years his elder, returned from America to live out his days. He had gone to America to work in the coal mines of western Pennsylvania and had earned enough money to take cor-respondence courses in law. Then, working as an attorney in New York City over five decades, he amassed a small fortune. However, he lost nearly all of it when stocks plummeted in the Panic of 1893.

During Nolan's youth, he would visit his aged great uncle, who instilled in him a love of America and a thirst for its opportunities. And when Sheenagh reached her eighteenth birthday and their families finally gave Nolan, who was twenty-two, permission to talk of marriage, it was his great uncle who most influenced the plans they made to go to America. He saw the boy as his personal project, constantly giving him advice.

"Take a cooked goose, hard cheeses, and two loaves of brown bread because you won't be able to eat what they give you on the ocean liner."

"Be the first to board the ship and pick out for yourself the very first bed at the bottom of the steps you descend. And if it's a bunk, take the bottom one because all the smells linger on top."

"In America, they select workers like they choose beasts in the market. If you're strong and healthy, that's all they care about. Remember, what you earn in America in a week, it will take you a month or longer to earn in Ireland."

Nolan's plan was to make the crossing, to earn enough to bring Sheenagh over, then to marry her.

He finally sailed in early 1914 and was able to pay for Sheenagh's crossing aboard the SS *Peterborough* in February 1915. The day after she landed safely in New York, they were married at City Hall. The bond was solemnized at St. Patrick's Cathedral a week later.

They took trolleys to the armory, a massive brick and stone structure that resembled a medieval castle. A crowd of several hundred people, almost entirely women, filled the street as they arrived. When the front doors were finally flung open, the crush of people frantic to get in made Nolan wonder if the stampede would turn dangerous. He intended to make Sheenagh wait, but when he looked over, she had already joined the moving herd.

The great drill hall of the armory was set up with rows of stalls where vendors had created miniature shops. Nolan spotted his wife sorting through a box holding tiny pairs of socks. He also spotted a corner of the room where the few men were congregating. The husbands' corner.

"Dear, I'll be over there," he said, pointing.

Besides food vendors and a newsstand, the corner had a public pay telephone. Nolan bought the *Sunday Daily Eagle* and got in line for the telephone.

Most of the headlines were about the war in Europe. "British Submarine Sinks an Austrian Seaplane and Torpedo Boat Convoy." However, one front-page story was about an escaped German spy recaptured on Broadway in Manhattan, just as the theaters were emptying after dinner.

Finally, the telephone was free. Nolan had the number and a nickel ready. Sean picked up on first bell.

"Tierney detective agency."

"Sean, this is John. I took a chance you'd be in."

"I got some boys in here that I'm sending over to Staten Island for something. But I got the message you left with my girl a coupla hours ago. So you found what you were looking for in the accounts. Good work, cousin."

"Yes, but there was more than I told your woman. The money Schulz is embezzling is going to a German man what's giving speeches around the city against America getting into the war. Fiery speeches. He's giving another tomorrow night. This money could be for all the bombings and sabotage and such that's been going on."

"None of my business. I got paid for you to find the man's accounting fraud. What he uses the money for is someone else's problem."

"Sean, one of us should be there tomorrow night to find out what this is all about."

"No one is stopping you."

"This isn't my case though. It's yours. Don't you care what this man is —"

"Cousin, I couldn't care less what he's doing with the money – unless someone is paying me to care."

"Then maybe we should call someone, federal agents or someone, and let them know about this."

"You're standing at a phone. Go ahead. But I got these boys standing here what needs revolvers for Staten Island. Gotta go, cousin."

Nolan hung up and sat on a bench to look again at the *Daily Eagle*. The story about the German spy said three federal Secret Service agents captured the man. Nolan went to the back of the line for the telephone, intending to ask a central operator if a federal office for the Secret Service existed in Manhattan. However, Sheenagh touched his shoulder from behind. "You have to come look at something."

He followed her up an aisle to a stall selling bassinets. She pointed to one hanging by a hook. "It's seventeen dollars, but it's got hem-stitched sheets and an embroidered coverlet. I know it's a little much, but can we afford it?"

He did not answer, which he hoped would be an answer.

"John? Can we?"

"I … I'm not sure, Sheenagh. That's nearly a week's pay and we have bills at —"

She frowned and walked away before he even finished. He watched her stop farther up the aisle and sort through flannel blankets, yanking one then another off the pile and feeling the fabric, her back to him. He knew when she was angry.

He thought a second then walked over to her.

"I called Sean and he offered me fifteen dollars for one more job. All I have to do is go see a German man speak tomorrow evening in Manhattan and write down what he says. I'll call him back and say I'll do it for you and this bassinet, dear. Here. Fifteen dollars."

She took it, smiled warmly and kissed his cheek. "You darling man. Thank you. Go back to your newspaper. I'll find you. But you promise, detective work is done after this. Agreed?"

He nodded, but feeling a thrill to be on a case again, he was not sure he meant it.

Riding on the subway

6

The Rally

THE FOLLOWING DAY, a Monday, Nolan left work at six o'clock and hurried uptown on a subway. He planned to get what information he could at the rally, then pass everything he learned to the city police or the Secret Service.

Rattling along beneath the city, he had to wonder. Why was he doing it? What was the urge he felt to look into this on his own, with no one paying him? Was he becoming a patriotic American, even without citizenship?

He realized that was exactly what it was. He wanted to do something good for his new country before he finally disappeared into the tedious anonymity of his office job – and preventing a bombing was something good.

The German Club, the Deutscher Verein, was a five-story building with a huge bronze eagle sitting atop the roof, looking regally over West 59th Street and Central Park.

On the sidewalk out front, as snow flurries flew in the chill air, men held tins to collect coins for the widows and children of dead German and Austrian soldiers. Nolan could hear a band, including a tuba, playing marches inside.

Fortunately, the crowds going in were large enough that the rally was delayed, so he had missed nothing. As he reached the door, a rough-looking man grabbed his arm.

"What's da business you got here?"

"I came for the speaker, Kohler."

"You're Irish, so okay, you go in. Glad you come, friend."

He was handed a program, but much of it was written in German. He saw Kohler's name, though. He also saw the name O'Leary, president of the American Irish Society.

Opinions about the war among the Irish in New York were split. Many felt that to rid Ireland of British rule, one had to support Germany. Others felt that if Germany overran England, it would overrun Ireland as well, then Irish culture would be lost forever. Nolan agreed with the latter. He never forgot something his father once wrote him. "England is the devil you know. Germany is the devil you don't know, so it's them I fear more."

The crowd moved as one into a ballroom in the rear of the first floor, set up with rows of wooden benches. Cigar smoke had already created a cloud-like haze over the room. Nolan could only find standing room near the rear.

A man on the podium at the front of the hall gaveled the rally to order by bringing his boot down hard on the

wooden platform several times. He motioned everyone
to stand, and with that, singing began. Nolan glanced at
the program. *"Deutschland Ueber Alles, Deutsche
Nationalhymne."* Nolan knew it to be the German national anthem. Men had hands on their hearts, others had
hands raised in salute. To not seem out of place, Nolan
pretended to sing.

Cheering followed, then the man with the boot raised
both hands to quiet the crowd. His German accent was
thick and his English poor.

"We going to run this in English for da Germans
attending who has speaked only English for so long. But
your mother tongue – as good Germans you must learn
it. Also, ve have guests who not be German but dey be
true friends of Germany."

Introductions of the men on the podium were made,
O'Leary among them. When an Illinois congressman
who favored American isolation was named, he rushed to
the front of the platform. "Only Germany supported us
in the Civil War! Not England! Not France!" Cheering
erupted throughout the hall.

The man with the boot came forward and quieted the
crowd. "In ten minutes ve start. Herr Kohler had to go to
da bathroom. Turn to the man next to you, say your
name, greet him as your friend."

Nolan was assailed from all sides. He immediately
invented a name. "James O'Connell, pleased to meet you
…James O'Connell … Yes, Ireland …James O'Connell,
how are you?."

The man on his right – Baumann if he heard correct-
ly – kept up the conversation, though, asking him about
his background with a slight German accent, perhaps

inherited from parents who were native Germans. Nolan invented details. Came over in 1914, a railroad worker, single, a rooming house in the Hell's Kitchen district.

Appearing to be in his forties, Baumann had a hawk-like profile, curly brown hair, and wire-rimmed spectacles, which he adjusted constantly as he listened, apparently a habit.

"What's your feeling about the war, my good Irish friend?" He asked

"Just what you'd expect," Nolan said. "That's why I'm here. Let me ask, what is being done to keep America out of the war? Can I help?"

"Can you help?" Baumann seemed to weigh how much to confide him. "I'm … I'm not sure at the moment."

"I work on the railroads. There must be something involving the railroads."

"We'll see, my friend. Just be patient." Baumann shook Nolan's hand then moved away, disappearing into the crowd.

Nolan engaged the man to his left, asking what was being done to convince America to stay out of the war. The man, who was Irish, perhaps newer to America than Nolan judging from his pants so far off his boot, unabashedly bragged to him about plots and schemes that "I personally have knowledge of."

"You watch. In the next couple of days you're going to hear about a lighter sinking in the Hudson loaded with horses and mules coming down to the city on their way to France. Just keep reading the newspapers."

"Can I be of any help? I work on the railroads."

"Ask around. Some of the boys might have something

for you. There's rumors of something big coming. Maybe railroads will be part of it, if you're lucky."

Just then, Kohler appeared. Tall and gaunt, he stood motionless with folded arms at the front of the podium. After the cheering stopped, the room turned solemn as he began to speak.

"Germany's victory will be soon if America stays out," Kohler said. "The English army cannot be reinforced as fast as their generals expected and the poor product they are sending to the front is only food for the German cannon. So our job in America is to keep America out permanently."

Again, cheering filled the room. Nolan had heard enough. Applauding with everyone else, he slowly backed out of the hall.

On the street, he looked for a trolley. However, further up 59th Street, which ran along Central Park, he saw two unmarked motors he knew belonged to the police department, one disguised as a bread truck. He also saw a detective he knew from another case, Jack Baker, leaning against an electric light pole.

He walked in that direction. As he got close to Baker and was recognized, Nolan motioned to him to stay quiet and to follow him into the park. Nolan kept walking and heard Baker's footsteps behind him.

They entered the park from Fifth Avenue and moved out of sight behind a gate.

"You were in the German Club. Why?" Baker asked him.

"I'm on a case, but I have some information for you."

Nolan told him the entire story. Cabot and Schulz, the embezzlement, the call to Kohler, the rumor inside about sabotage of a barge carrying horses and mules.

Baker wrote down the details. "I appreciate this. Where can we get in touch with you if we need to ask you more?"

Nolan gave him his address and telephone number in Brooklyn and his work address at Demers & Demers.

"But I'm an accountant now, Jack. My wife's going to have a baby, so I'm out of the business. Don't count on me for much."

Called in for a talk

7

Undercover

A WEEK LATER, on February first, Nolan was at his desk working when three men walked into Demers & Demers – two in freshly pressed suits and one in a police uniform. Their stride up the aisle was so officious that everyone in the room turned.

They walked forward to the enclosed office of Edward Demers and were quickly let in.

Nolan went back to his accounting, but in a minute, the secretary for Demers tapped his shoulder. "Mr. Demers wants to talk to you."

What had he done? His heart racing, he walked into Demers' office. "You asked to see me?"

One of the three men turned to Demers. "We'd like to speak to him in private, if you don't mind."

"If he's done something, I want to know about it," Demers said.

"He hasn't done anything. This is about something we're going to ask him to do."

Reluctantly, Demers left, closing the door behind him.

"John Nolan, I'm Captain Thomas Tunney of the New York City Bomb Squad."

"Roger Wood, Assistant United States Attorney, the Department of Justice."

"Byron Pickerell, the Treasury."

"This is our problem," said Tunney, who was tall and square-jawed with piercing eyes and a no-nonsense quality. "We have too many people in our departments who side with the Germans, so these pro-German plotters in the city responsible for some of these bombings quickly find out who our undercover men are. We need someone from the outside to do a job we've got, someone unknown in any of our departments."

"We heard you passed along some good information about these German groups to one of the city's detectives," Wood said. "He vouches for you, says you're very sharp."

"What's the job?" Nolan asked.

"There's rumors," Tunney said, glancing at the others. "Rumors from British intelligence that something is in the works, maybe bombings in our city. The rumor is that a German, a man trained with a new type of explosive, is on his way to New York. We can only guess what that'll be for."

"So you want me to go undercover for you."

"Yes."

Nolan shook his head. "With all respect, I'm not a detective anymore. My wife —"

"We know. You've got a baby coming," Tunney said, "But we wouldn't be here if it wasn't important, very important."

Tunney, who had an air of impatience, of having to be somewhere else in ten minutes, sat on the corner of Demers' desk and eyed Nolan. "Let me ask you," he said. "What if you didn't help us? Then these people blow up a bomb in Pennsylvania Station, killing hundreds. Then you was to read about this in the papers, knowing you didn't help. How would that make you feel? Ask yourself?"

Nolan sighed, knowing he could not get out of it now. His conscience had him cornered as much as these men.

"What about my job, my paycheck?"

"How much does Demers pay you?" Wood asked.

"Twenty-five a week."

The three men traded glances.

"We can scrape up forty between us, can't we gentlemen, plus expenses?" Wood said. "I know Eddie Demers. He served on the Governor's Council. I'll get him to give you leave for two or three months."

"That's all this will take? Two or three months?"

"Yes. That's what we're hearing."

Tunney outlined the plan. They would rent Nolan an apartment in an Irish neighborhood on the West Side, in Hell's Kitchen, under a different name. ("You'd only have to stay there two nights of every three. The other, you can go home to your wife.") They would get him proper identity papers and find him a job. He would get to know people in the neighborhood, attend pro-German meetings, and try to work his way into the group planning the bombings.

"I'll give you the private number to my desk," Tunney said. "Anytime you have something, you call me direct … So that's our problem, John. Can you do it?"

Tunney gazed at Nolan, waiting for an answer, until he reluctantly nodded.

"Just one thing," Nolan said. "You have to convince my wife first. That'll be the hard part."

Tunney thought a moment. "I have a good friend, a former official in the police department. He's very persuasive. You give me a time to come by to talk to your wife in a few days and we'll be there."

Capt. Tunney arrives to convince Sheenagh

8

Sheenagh Listens

DRYING DISHES AFTER dinner, Sheenagh came to the door between the kitchen and front room, a rag and plate in hand. "John, who are these men that you keep looking for out the window?"

"Just friends. They want to meet you."

In a few minutes, he spotted Tunney and another man turn the corner onto Clinton Avenue, stepping around the piles of fresh snow on the sidewalk.

He went out to the hallway and opened the front door for them. "I didn't tell her why you're here, so that's your job," he said.

Inside, the men shook off the snow and hung their coats. Nolan went to the kitchen door.

"Sheenagh, they're here."

"In a minute. Let —"

"Sheenagh, please. Come on out."

He walked back into the front room and for the first time saw the other man's face. He froze.

Sheenagh, wiping her wet hands on her apron, came out smiling.

"You must be John's wife," Tunney said. "I'm Tom Tunney, Captain Tunney, of the New York City Police Department. So nice to make your acquaintance."

He crossed the room and shook her hand. Sheenagh turned to the other man and he stepped forward, offering his hand.

"And I'm Colonel Roosevelt," he said.

Nolan's heart was racing. The broad face, the mustache, the circular spectacles.

"You're a colonel, are you," Sheenagh said. "What are you colonel of? The military or the police?"

Nolan was about to tell her, but Tunney, holding in a laugh, touched his arm and shook his head.

"I … uh, I was a colonel in the military, dear. But twenty years ago, I was the city's police commissioner." Roosevelt was smiling, immensely pleased with the turn of the situation.

Sheenagh looked skeptical. "You're telling me you were the commissioner, the commissioner of the entire police department?"

"I was head of the Board of Police Commissioners, yes."

Now she seemed to understand something serious was going on. The front room had a wide sofa and two armchairs. She took a seat in one of the armchairs and everyone else found a place. For the next half hour, the two men told her of their problem, the rumors about the bombing plot and the agent being sent by Germany just for this mission, their need for an undercover man from outside the department, the recommendation of John by several sources.

Sheenagh's expression remained hard, her mouth tight, through it all, but Nolan knew that meant nothing other than she was giving it all her attention.

Finally, they paused and Tunney asked her what she thought.

"If John does this, when we stand for citizenship in three years, will you give us your recommendations?"

Tunney nodded. "I sincerely promise I will."

She looked at the other man, and Roosevelt leaned forward. "Dear, I'll personally speak to the president of the United States himself in support of your application. And that I promise too."

"That's quite a boast," she said. "You're telling me you know the president of these United States?"

"My dear," Tunney said. "Colonel Roosevelt was the president of the United States. This is Theodore Roosevelt. He lives outside the city on Long Island, and he's a great friend of the city's police."

Sheenagh stared at Roosevelt in stunned silence for a moment, saw the smiles on the other faces, then suddenly burst into tears. It took ten minutes for Nolan and Roosevelt to console her enough that she would stop crying.

In the end, she agreed, but she requested that the former president sign a photograph of her mother and father to send to them.

"And here. I want you both to take a slice of my lemon pie. Please."

A fire truck races by

9

Preparation

RETURNING TO GLASGOW on February four-teenth, twelve days before the *Bristol Star* was to sail, Schwegel found a room in the Carlisle Hotel three blocks off Prince's Dock.

Abteilung IIIb had given him two thousand pounds, a steamer trunk with a hidden compartment, and vari-ous forged papers to establish his identity as a sales agent for Deecks & Co. He registered at the hotel as McFee, believing it was unlikely he would run into any-one who would recognize him, especially if he stayed to his room. And he planned to. While at home, he had visited a travel bookshop and purchased books about American life and culture, which he wanted to read while waiting for the sailing.

Most importantly, though, he wanted to work on the bomb design and the mission plan.

A year earlier, a group of German nationals in New York City had attempted to bomb ships loaded with munitions and other war supplies on their way to England. They were arrested before any damage was done. However, their bomb design still intrigued German intelligence.

It was created by a German infantry officer who had passed it along to army intelligence in Berlin. It was a time bomb in a watertight container that would be attached to a ship's hull on the rudder post. Each swing of the rudder would turn a beveled wheel in the bomb by one notch. Eventually, the wheel would turn enough revolutions to trigger the explosives, TNT, and blow a hole in the ship's hull, sinking it.

The bombs were to be attached near the ship's rudder above the water line before the ship was loaded. Then, as the cargo was brought on, the ship would settle lower and the bomb would disappear below the surface of the water so that it would not be seen as the ship passed out of the harbor.

When he was first sent back to Scotland by Abteilung IIIb, as a cover, Schwegel took a graduate chemistry course at University of Glasgow. However, his real job was to monitor munitions factories and shipbuilding companies. And twice he acted as a courier to bring captured British papers back to Berlin via the Netherlands.

On the second trip, his immediate supervisor in Berlin happened to show him the design for the rudder bomb.

"The problem is that the Americans now know about this bomb," the supervisor said. "So they will start inspecting the rudders of ships lying in the harbor. Too bad. It might have worked well."

Schwegel studied the design as the supervisor lit a pipe.

"Magnets," Schwegel said. "Magnets will save this."

He told of seeing a preliminary paper written by a Japanese researcher concerning new metal alloys that could make magnets smaller and more powerful.

"It relies on cobalt added to tungsten steel. Quite strong. You could send divers down to stick such a bomb onto the hull well out of sight. It wouldn't have to be attached to the rudder. There are better timing devices out there, I'm sure."

He stayed in Berlin and began work with design engineers in German intelligence to create a smaller bomb but with enough power to blow a hole in a ship's hull. While this was being done, a local foundry created ten sample magnets of the new alloy.

Over several days, a single bomb of the new design was fashioned, and at dusk one evening a diver attached it three meters below the water line of the hull of an empty, rusting freighter at anchor on the Havel River in Berlin.

The detonation was timed for noon the following day, and it came at four minutes past the hour. Owing to the bomb's depth below water, the explosion was barely heard from the shore, where a dozen German military officials and Schwegel observed. Nevertheless, the freighter sank in under ten minutes and the ambitious plot that now brought him back to Glasgow was set in motion.

The current plan of the German military was to put all the bombs in place the day prior to Easter. They would be timed to explode as close to simultaneously as possible at noon on April twenty-third when churches had let out and people swarmed Fifth Avenue as part of the annual Easter Parade.

German officials who devised the mission believed the crowds would hear the explosions and see the rising plumes of smoke in the harbor and elsewhere in the city. It would convince them. The war could come to them, it could land right on their doorstep, if America chose to fight. The battlefields would not be just across an ocean in Europe.

On Easter morning, letters would be posted to all the major newspapers in the city and would arrive in the days after the explosions – a manifesto of the saboteurs' intentions, a warning to America to stay out of the war.

In his hotel room, he took two papers from his trunk's hidden compartment and laid them on the bed side by side. One was the bomb design on blue drafting paper. The other was a list of chemical supplies he would need.

He hoped that by staring at the two papers, his thinking would clear about what lay ahead and his resolve would deepen.

❦

"What's the fish tonight?" he asked the waiter.

"Sea bass."

"I'll try that and the crab salad," he said, handing back the menu.

Schwegel was dining in a seafood restaurant across the street from the hotel. The faint alarm bells that had been sounding for the past minute only now caught his attention. Suddenly, a horse-drawn fire truck raced by the window, and like other patrons, he stood to see more, only mildly curious at that point.

However, at the restaurant's door, he saw smoke coming out a window on the third floor of the hotel, a floor above his. A surge of fear went suddenly went through him. His bomb design and list of chemicals were still sitting on his bed. They could be discovered by a fireman or destroyed completely.

Seeing firemen entering the building with axes, he rushed across the street. Two policemen stopped him at the door.

"But I'm registered. I need to save my belongings."

"Wait on the sidewalk. When it's safe, we'll let you up."

Frantic, Schwegel went down an alley to the rear of the hotel. The service door was unguarded and he rushed in and climbed the service stairs to his floor. Thick black smoke lingered near the hallway ceiling, so he began crawling toward his room. However, a black-helmeted fireman entered the hall from the main stairs.

"What's going on here? No one is allowed in the hotel. I could have you arrested. Are you a looter?"

"I … I have to get to my room. My belongings. I can't lose them. I'm a man who obtains contracts for foundries. I'm on my way to Canada to procure war contracts. I can show you my papers."

The smoke was clearing, rapidly exiting the hall from broken windows on each end. The fireman, younger than himself, removed his helmet and wiped the sweat off his face with his sleeve. He seemed to accept Schwegel's story.

Thinking quickly, Schwegel said, "Thank you for saving the hotel."

The fireman, unbuttoning his heavy black rubber coat, smiled broadly. Schwegel immediately knew any danger had passed.

"You know what it was," the fireman said. "A woman wanted to be arrested, so she got her room, put her sweater in a trashcan, lit it on fire, and waited." He turned to the stairs to leave, then glanced back. "Said she was tired of her husband and her children and cooking and cleaning all day and wanted to go spend some time in jail as a rest."

Schwegel laughed, as much from relief as from the humor of it. "Then well done by everyone. You saved the hotel and she got her vacation."

Accosted on the street

10

Hell's Kitchen

NOLAN LEASED A dingy one-bedroom apartment in a tenement on West 51st Street in the heart of Hell's Kitchen, the notorious Irish neighborhood that spawned the Gopher Gang, the Parlor Mob, and other criminal organizations. Eighteen dollars a month, peeling wallpaper on every wall, floors so covered with grime and grease that you could barely see the wood beneath, a coal stove in the kitchen, a common bathroom in the hall.

He furnished it with items given to him by Tunney from the department's confiscated property room, including an iron bed and a kitchen table. By the time a hired cart got all the furniture to the apartment, it was nearly midnight.

Nolan's first year in America was spent living in a tenement no better than this on 106th Street, trying to save money to bring Sheenagh over, doing little in his life but work, eat, and sleep. It was a grueling, often depressing existence, for much of the time. As teeming with people as Manhattan was, it was a city that could make a person lonely, especially an immigrant living alone who had been surrounded by family his entire life.

Sheenagh had washed their spare set of bed sheets in lavender soap for him. He put them on the bed as well as two wool blankets and a feather pillow, doused the kerosene lamp, undressed, and tried to sleep. He could not. It was more than the noise – motor horns outside, men arguing on the sidewalk, a baby crying elsewhere in the building. He was sharply aware that this was the first night he had slept apart from Sheenagh in more than a year.

In Brooklyn, he would have been able to open his eyes in the night, and in the deflected street light coming through their bedroom window from the alley, he would have seen her comforting form under the blankets, heard her light breathing, been able to reach over and touch her. Now he saw nothing on the other side of the bed and it emptied him.

He almost felt as if he were back on 106th Street, back in that desolate life, and the intervening year of wedded happiness had never happened.

—◆—

"Where are you calling from?" Sheenagh asked.

"From a public phone in a hotel. I only have a minute. The flat is on 51st. It's awful but I guess it's good enough."

"And you'll come home—"

"Every third night. I'll try to call at noon on the second day. That way, we'll talk every day."

"And like I asked, you'll look for a church."

"Yes, and like I asked, you'll stay upstairs with the

Shapiros the nights I'm not there."

"They're happy to have me … John, I miss you already."

Something about the soft way she said it emptied him. He had to keep himself from tearing up. "Sheenagh, I feel the same."

He heard her gasping breathing and knew she was crying.

"I'll … I'll see you tomorrow night, John. The key is in the hall. You know where."

"I love you, dear. I've got to go."

———◆≥◆———

Nolan had begun to grow a beard to disguise himself and to have the rough look that would fit his new job. On his first morning as O'Connell, he walked the neighborhood, looking for a church.

He had promised Sheenagh that if he stayed in his Hell's Kitchen apartment overnight on a Saturday, he would go to Mass Sunday morning in the neighborhood.

In an Irish neighborhood, he did not have to walk far to find a Catholic church. Sacred Heart of Jesus on West 51st, near Tenth Avenue.

Not that he planned to attend its Sunday Mass. He only wanted to present a convincing lie to Sheenagh when she asked if he had. He learned in his youth that the advice of priests and nuns was suspect at best, harmful at worst. Instead, he had learned to rely on his own instincts and feelings of right and wrong to navigate the world. Eventually, he grew to mistrust anyone – or any institution – that tried to impose their thinking on him. However, Sheenagh was still drawn to the church and he wanted always to please her, so at home, he attended with her.

Later, Nolan walked 51st Street, learning his neighborhood stores, as snow flurries began to coat the sidewalks. As he came out of McCurdy's Market with a bag of groceries, he was approached by two men in derbies and identical fur-collared overcoats. Both were about his age but smaller in stature.

"You mind we talk to you?" one asked, his Irish accent as thick as any Nolan had ever heard. "You're new in the district. You interested in playing a raffle? Two bits and you get five tickets."

"No thanks. I don't got two bits to spare."

"Sure you do. Everyone's got two bits. Check your pockets."

Seeming to find courage in their superior number, they crowded closer around him. Nolan knew how this was going to go, and from his experience in fights, he knew if he caught one of them fast, a sharp kick to the knee, the other would think twice about jumping in, being the only one left to fight. Nolan pulled his right leg back slowly and waited for the moment.

"I'm being honest. I spent my last two bits on this bag."

"You give us the bag, Mick, and we'll give you the tickets," the smaller of the two men said, taking a step even closer.

Nolan swung his leg as rapidly as he could at this man, catching him with his boot on the side of his left knee and sending him tumbling to the sidewalk in pain. The other man froze, seeing the angry resolve in Nolan's eye.

"If I put down this bag," Nolan told him, "it's because I'm going to get serious about this fight. You want me to get serious?"

The man backed away.

"Why the hell did you do that?" whined the man on the sidewalk, rubbing his knee.

"'You would have done me worse if I didn't do you first,' we used to say growing up. But let me ask you," Nolan said to the standing man. "I've just moved here from Boston for a railroad job. I don't know anyone, though. Is there an Irish social club around here where a man could meet his neighbors?"

"I'm your neighbor," the standing man said. "I saw you come out of the corner apartments."

"You live in the same building? What's your name?"

"You think I'm gonna give you my name?"

The man on the sidewalk tentatively stood. "There's an Irish club on 46th at Eighth Avenue but its for the old-timers. We weren't lying, though. There is a raffle. For the war fund. What side you on?"

"The Irish side," Nolan said.

"England or Germany?"

"Not England," Nolan said. "Does that count against me?"

"It counts for you," the man who had been kicked said, still massaging his knee. "Maybe if we see you again, we can treat you better. Although you're not the one got treated bad here, are you?"

⎯⎯⎯❦⎯⎯⎯

At six o'clock, Nolan walked down to 46th Street and saw a growing crowd of men gathered near Eighth Avenue. However, he saw neither of the men from earlier in the afternoon. He did see the German who had questioned him at the rally, though. Baumann was it?

Nolan re-introduced himself. "Remember me? O'Connell?"

"O'Connell, glad to have you with us." He offered his hand. "Henrik Baumann."

Nolan took it. "With you for what?"

However, the German did not hear him, as several in the crowd had started shouting toward a doorway. Nolan glanced up to where a sign was draped from the eaves of the third floor. Irish American League of New York.

Glancing back, Nolan saw a police wagon turning onto the street from Eighth Avenue. Then he saw another wagon enter the other end at Ninth. Both ends were blocked. Suddenly in front of him, a rock was thrown at a window, shattering it, and policemen were spilling out of the wagons, nightsticks in hand.

⁕

"Says your name's O'Connell. But you got no address," said the detective, holding Nolan's identity papers. They were in an interrogation room of the 51st Street Precinct. Cement floors, white-washed walls with peeling paint, bare overhead lights. Nolan sat in a wooden chair, his hands shackled in front of him, as a detective stood over him.

"I just rented an apartment today. I moved down from Boston for employment."

"Employment where?"

"I'm supposed to report tomorrow to the Sunnyside rail yards. I was just out walking in the neighborhood when I saw the crowd and got curious."

Nolan was resolved not to mention his undercover work or Tunney's name. He had no idea who this detective was or who he would talk to.

"So your story is you was in the wrong place at the wrong time.

"Sometimes it's an honest story."

"Sometimes it ain't. Did you know the crowd was German?"

"All I know is it was a crowd and I was curious."

"I don't believe you."

"It's the truth."

The detective punched him in the ear, a sharp sudden blow. Then he gazed at Nolan as if the punch was going to bring out a different story. Nolan sat still in the chair and looked only at the cement floor.

"Let me ask you, O'Connell. These German bombings in the city. You have any part in any of that?"

"I'm Irish, not German. I just work on the railroad."

"Some Irishman seem to think they're German."

His ear hurt so bad that Nolan had to rub it with his shackled hands. There was blood on his palm when he took it away.

"I just wanted to see the neighborhood was all."

"Idiot Mick." The detective went to the interrogation room door. "Put him back in the cell. Bring me another."

⚬

Nolan's ear was still bleeding when he arrived back in the holding cell, where about a dozen men from the 46th Street crowd waited. Baumann came over. Nolan saw one of the small men who had confronted him on the street in the afternoon.

Baumann handed him a handkerchief. "What'd they ask you?"

"My name and why I was in the crowd," Nolan said.

"What'd you tell them?"

The small man came over, the one he had not kicked.

"Just my name and that was all," Nolan said.

"Why'd you get hit?" Baumann asked.

"He asked me if I backed England in the war. I guess he didn't like my answer. "

The small man laughed. "I bet you wished you could have hit him back. You woulda done it too, I bet, if you got the chance. Henrik, this man's a good fighter. I seen firsthand. My name's O'Keefe, by the way."

⸺⸱⸻⸱⸺

Nolan read about the arrests the next morning in the *Herald*.

IRISH TURN ON IRISH

Protest at Irish-American Meeting

About a dozen Irishmen and perhaps as many Germans were arrested outside the meeting hall of the Irish American League of New York on 46th Street yesterday after being denied admission to the meeting.

Inside, the league's governing council voted unanimously to back a position in support of President Wilson and the Allied cause.

The crowd of men, prevented from entering the hall by armed guards, instead took their protest to the sidewalk,

denouncing the President and Dublin while shouting support for Germany and the Teutonic confederation.

The disturbance was growing danger- ous, with stones being tossed, when police reserves arrived to quell the bud- ding riot.

Toward the end of the story, there was a list of those arrested, including him.

James O'Connell, address unknown.

However, Nolan underlined two other names.

Henrik Baumann, 331 E. 86th Street
Paul R. O'Keefe, 301 W. 51st Street.

Two Pigeons Tavern

11

The Sunnyside Train Yard

THE FORGED PAPERS Tunney got him were, as requested, for James O'Connell, twenty-nine, a railroad switchman, previously employed in Boston.

"We planted records for you in Boston to support your story. You report Wednesday morning to the Sunnyside train yard in Long Island City," Tunney had told him. "Ask for a man named Tunney, and yes, I know him. He's my cousin and he runs the yard."

Nolan closed the shed door behind him to keep out the blowing snow. Other trainmen packed the room, crowding around a coal stove that pumped out heat.

"Who're you?" one of the trainmen asked him.

"I'm supposed to report to Mr. Tunney."

"He ain't in yet. This your first day?"

"First day in this yard," Nolan said, brushing the snow off his jacket. "Before this, I worked up in Massachusetts for the Boston and Maine."

Other trainmen entered the shed, the snow flying in after them. They were all waiting for their assignments from Tunney whose empty desk sat by the window.

Nolan had forgotten to bring his heavy rubber boots with him from Brooklyn. In his leather hobnail boots, his feet were going to get soaked and frozen.

The door opened again, with more snow flying, and a man walked in that did not resemble the Captain Tunney he knew. However, from the way everyone turned and deferred to him, it had to be the Tunney who employed them.

"Gentlemen, I hope you ate a good breakfast," this Tunney said. "We're gonna do some work today. You're all going on shovel details."

Tracks, trestles, and bridges around the city had to be cleared of the deepening snow, he said. He took a chair at the desk and began taking names and giving out assignments. The Jamaica Bay trestle, the Queensborough Bridge, the Vernon Avenue Bridge.

Nolan finally reached the front of the line.

"Name?"

"James O'Connell."

Tunney looked up from his ledger. "Stand over there, O'Connell. I'll get to you."

Fifteen minutes later, the shed empty except for the two of them, Tunney stood.

"As long as you work for me, never mention my cousin and never talk to me directly except about work. I'll assign you something if you come in, but from what I've been told, there are days you won't be coming in. Don't tell me anything about anything. You understand?"

"Yes, sir."

"I don't want no grand jury calling me to find out what I know about this. Understand?"

"Yes sir, but what if —"

"See? You're already breaking my rule and trying to tell me something about something. I don't want to know nothing about nothing. Go get a shovel and find Harrison outside, one of the crew chiefs. You're going down to Vernon Avenue. And get some snow boots or you'll lose your toes to frostbite."

⁕

Ten hours later, Nolan sat exhausted at a table in the Two Pigeons Tavern on 48th Street, a block from his apartment. The roasted chicken in front of him had been reduced to its bones, and the roasted potatoes had vanished. An empty glass that had held beer was in front of him and a second half-filled glass in his hand was about to join it.

Out of the corner of his vision, Nolan had been watching Paul O'Keefe sitting at the bar, the man from his building who had accosted him on the street and been arrested with him later. One thing he noticed was O'Keefe had glanced into the mirror behind the bar several times to see Nolan.

As Nolan rose to pay his tab and go back to his apartment, O'Keefe got off his bar stool and walked over.

"O'Connell. Can I talk to you?"

"If you want."

"Please. Sit back down a second. You know anything about the railroad lines through New Jersey?"

"A few things."

O'Keefe leaned in close. "You know anything about the du Pont plant down near Penns Grove in New

Jersey?"

Nolan shook his head.

"It's down on the Delaware River. They make powder for explosives what gets shipped up to New York by train along with cannon shells. Then it all goes onto freighters headed for England. What I'm wondering is can you get information about the train shipments?"

"You mean when they are scheduled?"

"When and what routes."

"I doubt it. They'd keep something like that secret."

"Of course it's secret. If it wasn't secret, I would already know when these trains run. That's why I'm asking you. There's some boys that wants to prevent that shipment from making it to New York."

"Prevent it how?"

"A bomb on the tracks."

"What is it you're asking me exactly?"

"The schedule for the next train shipment."

"Like I said. I doubt I can get it."

"Try," O'Keefe said, then he got up and left.

Someone picked up the telephone on first bell. "Who's this?" A voice asked.

"I, uh, I was calling for Captain Tunney," Nolan said. He was at the public phone in the Hotel Flanders on Broadway.

"What I asked is – who's this?"

"John Nolan."

"John, good. What do you got for me?"

"I was approached by one of the Irishmen working for the Germans. He's not one of the important men, and I don't know how much he knows. But he wants me to find out when the next du Pont munitions train is scheduled to go from Penns Grove in New Jersey up to the docks on New York Harbor. They want to dynamite the tracks to either derail it or blow it up. If I want to get into their ring and meet the men higher up, it sounds like I better come up with something for him."

Tunney thought a moment. "Call me back tomorrow night, the same time, and I'll have a plan."

———⋙———

The information Nolan gave O'Keefe two days later, based on Tunney's plan, was this. A munitions train would depart the du Pont siding at ten o'clock Friday morning, March third, and travel on the secondary railroad lines north to the Jersey City piers where the cargo was to be loaded onto a waiting freighter.

"They mainly patrol the rail lines north of Camden," Nolan told O'Keefe. "If they want to stop that shipment, the best spot is when the tracks pass through a section of scrublands twelve miles northeast of Penns Grove near Swedesboro. They never patrol that section. There's only one dirt road that goes back in there, Cole Farm Road. Tell these men to go to the end of that road where it stops at the tracks and that's where they should set their dynamite. But they should use a fuse and get out before it goes off. When it blows, people will hear it and police will trap them back in there. The train'll have a coal boiler. You tell them that when it derails, if they're lucky, the powder will explode in the fire."

What Nolan did not tell O'Keefe was this. The train would not be carrying barrels of powder and cannon shells, only police detectives and a crew to repair the blown rail.

The Bristol Star

12

The Departure

A SINGLE-FUNNEL, TWO-MASTED steamship, the *Bristol Star* was built in 1884 before the age of the behemoths of the ocean. At nearly four hundred feet, it was less than half the length of the largest steamers that were plying the Atlantic at the outbreak of the war – the *SS Vaterland* and the *SS Bismarck*. Nevertheless, it still had room for more than three hundred passengers, although fewer than eighty would cross in the relative luxury of first or second class. The rest would be huddled in the uncomfortable conditions of steerage.

On the day of his departure, Schwegel, carrying the passport of Robert McFee, arrived before noon at Prince's Dock rolling a single steamer trunk. The blue sky was cloudless, the late February air was chilly. The sunlight glinted off the silver rails of the ship, giving the scene the thrilling beauty steamship departures always seemed to have for him. Passengers on line chatting, baggage men at work, seagulls gliding overhead. It was as if there were no war going on, as if he were only going on a vacation.

With a lean face that seemed permanently without emotion, Schwegel had no difficulty hiding whatever nervousness he had. In fact, he was not sure he felt very nervous. Espionage was a cold business and since he began training for this mission, his emotions had been replaced with a kind of calculating resolve. Just get it done. Get it done for Austria and Germany and for the conclusion to this war.

On the pier, a team of uniformed inspectors checked passports and examined the contents of trunks, suitcases, and other luggage. With the boarding deadline still three hours away, the line of passengers waiting to climb the gangplank was short.

"Destination?" The inspector had his hand out.

Schwegel gave him his passport. "Halifax. On business."

"And what's your business, sir?"

"I'm a sales agent for Deecks and Company. We contract for the production of shell casings for our explosives. We hope to get contracts with foundries in Canada. Like everyone, there's a fear of the war and its effect on production here in Scotland."

"Says you're twenty-eight. What about military service? Aren't you going to serve?"

"Our business is war exempt. I've got a letter."

Schwegel handed over the forged paper on the letterhead of the Aberdeen Military Service Tribunal granting his personal exemption.

The inspector glanced at the letter then looked into Schwegel's face with a kind of professional suspicion. Just to test himself, Schwegel gazed back, attempting to show nothing except innocence of anything the man might be thinking. The two men held their gazes for a full five seconds, a duel of stares, until the inspector finally looked back at the letter, which Schwegel took to be satisfaction for what he had or had not seen.

"Have you heard anything about conditions at sea?" Schwegel boldly asked, an indication he was innocent enough to engage in chitchat with this inspector.

"You mean weather?"

"Actually, I mean the German submarines. Any danger expected on this crossing?"

"There's always danger, but right now the Germans are targeting freighters, not ships like this. You should be safe. Sir, I'm going to have to ask you to step aside for the moment."

This gave Schwegel a start. "Any problem?"

"Sir, just step aside."

When he attempted to carry his trunk with him, the inspector planted his hand on top of it to prevent him. "Just step aside, if you will."

Schwegel moved to the barrier and waited. He thought about drawing out a cigarette and smoking as evidence of his lack of concern. However, it might be conspicuous enough to register with a trained inspector that the opposite could also be true, that it might be an attempt to hide concern.

Then again, what were the chances any lowly paid pier inspector in Glasgow, Scotland, was cunning enough to think beyond the obvious? He drew out the Turkish cigarette, lit it, leaned against the wooden barrier, and stared off past the docked *Bristol Star*, at the river channel, busy at the moment with tugboats and fishing vessels.

The inspector spoke to two other men, uniformed police. He showed them McFee's passport, pointed to Schwegel, then moved to deal with the next passenger in line. The officers approached Schwegel.

"Sir, we'd like to ask you a question."

Schwegel dropped the cigarette and crushed it with his boot. "Go right ahead."

"Your passport says you have a scar on your chin. The inspector saw no such scar."

Schwegel lifted his chin and pointed to where he knew it was on the underside. "It's old enough that the skin has lightened. You have to look closely."

One officer bent down to examine, even placing a finger on the flesh of his throat. "That's no scar. It's a mark and that's all. How'd you get it?"

"Running through a forest when I was six. The end of a branch caught me," which was the truth.

"You can barely see it," the officer said. "Why the hell do they put things like that on passports? It just confuses everyone, gets people all excited."

Schwegel smiled as the officer pulled away his hand. "They asked about scars when I went into the registry for the passport and I told them. If I didn't and someone saw it, they might say, 'Why's this scar not on your passport?' Then I'd still be in trouble. So damned if you do, damned if you don't."

There was a momentary silence. Schwegel felt a bit of relief. The officers did not retreat, though.

"One other thing then, sir. Your trunk. It was made in Berlin. Why's that, sir?"

This sent a shiver of fear though Schwegel. He

thought he had considered every possibility. Not this, though. His mind raced to invent a story.

"Well, it wasn't originally mine. I don't make a great deal of money and don't travel a great deal, so I bought it second hand, through the newspaper."

"So it's used, then."

"It was when I bought it."

"Says manufactured in 1915, though. Treber Luggage in Berlin. Pretty new to be sold off as used."

"I ... I had no knowledge of its age when I bought it. All I knew was that a man wanted to get rid of it. I can't say why, although he did mention a death in the family. I never thought to look to see when it was made. Why would I? But that's good for me, isn't it. 1915. It just says the materials should hold up a bit longer than I expected."

"This man. Was he German?"

"He might have been. I ... I don't recall an accent. Perhaps the person who died was. I didn't think at the time to consider any of this. I needed a trunk and this was the one I could afford."

The two officers gazed into his face and Schwegel could think of no way to act but honestly. Concern at the questions.

"Sir, I'm going to ask you to think, as you make this crossing, about anything you do that could reflect aspects of this war. Having a German trunk is a thing you have to think about. But you can go on your way. Have a pleasant crossing."

They walked away, spoke briefly to the inspector who gestured to Schwegel to proceed aboard.

He picked up the trunk, set it onto its rollers and slowly began the climb up the gangplank. He quickly grew short of breath and light-headed despite the low angle of the climb. He knew his pulse was racing. He knew he was overcome by his near fatal mistake. Why had he not thought to examine the trunk? If the officers had asked him when he bought the trunk before telling him the date of its manufacture, he would likely have said four or five years ago. If so, he would have been done. He would be in handcuffs and on his way to jail.

Mistakes. They were too easy to make. He gritted his teeth as he continued on the climb. Spying was going to be a harder business than he thought.

First-class stateroom

13

Underway

SCHWEGEL KNEW HE could justifiably claim seasickness his first few days at sea to avoid eating his meals with other passengers, but he felt an excitement about finally being launched on his career as a spy. Being in Scotland, which he knew so well, was not espionage. Being at sea, on his way to Canada among strangers, was. And he wanted a good opportunity to test himself.

So opening his trunk in his first-class cabin – an iron bed, sitting bench, wash basin, and private bathroom – he took out his evening clothes and began to dress for dinner. As he did, he tried to eliminate the last shred of Peter Schwegel from his identity. He knew he had to think of himself entirely as McFee to get it over.

As a boy, he was slow to learn English until he was told a particular thing. His method had been to see a tree, think of the German word, *baum*, for tree, then ask himself what the English word was for baum. So to speak in English was an awkward and halting experience. Describing this to an instructor in his elementary school, he was told to eliminate the German middleman in his process. "*siehe Baum, denke* tree." See *baum*, think tree.

Now he stood before the tiny mirror above the wash basin and shaved. See Schwegel, think McFee.

———◆———

"I crossed on the *Olympic* in 1911. Quite the experience. It's so huge, so heavy, you don't realize you're moving. The waves can't move it. It moves the waves," said the Canadian farmer.

The dessert of fig pudding served, the coffee and tea coming, they sat around the largest table in the dining saloon – the British gentleman from London, the Canadian wheat farmer from Ontario and his wife, the Irish salesman from Cork and his wife, the American mathematics professor from Boston, and Schwegel, who was the youngest of the group by a decade at least.

"I heard they had a Turkish bath and a Roman bath," said the wife of the Irishman.

"I think it's the *Imperator* that has the Roman bath," the Canadian farmer said. "The *Olympic* has the Turkish bath, but it also has a saltwater swimming pool down in the bowels of the ship. It takes in and circulates fresh seawater constantly."

"Mr. McFee, we haven't heard much from you," said the American.

"I wouldn't have much to add. This is my first crossing."

"The Scottish accent. Isn't it wonderful," said the

wife of the Canadian farmer. "Yours is slight, though. I hear quite a bit of England in it, maybe some … What? Where are you from?"

"Scotland but I went to school in England, so that's why my Scottish is not so thick as some." At least, they heard no Austrian, he thought.

"You know," the American said. "When people in my country imitate you Scots, people who've never met a Scot, they roll their R's like this. Girrrrl. But no Scot I know does it that way. They say Girrl, a single repetition of the R."

"Give us a sample of some Scottish, Mr. McFee," said the Irish salesman. "Why don't you tell us something about yourself."

"Let's see. I'm from Edinburgh originally. I attended university in England, got my degree in chemistry, and now I'm on my way to Canada on business."

"War business?" asked the Irish salesman.

"Everything is war business at the moment, isn't it," Schwegel said.

There were solemn nods from the men. The two wives seemed to retreat from the conversation, seeing it as heading for the men's subject, the European war. The men around the table pushed away their plates and took up their cups of coffee or tea, preparing. They could have just as well have rolled up their sleeves, Schwegel thought with amusement.

"And what's your view of the conflict, Mr. McFee? I imagine as a Scot you fear being under the boot of the German," said the Canadian farmer.

"None of us want to be under the boot of anyone," said the Irish salesman. "I'm Irish and we've been under the boot of the English forever."

"Would a German boot be any better?" The British gentleman asked, a gruffness in his tone.

An awkward silence followed. The Canadian farmer turned to Schwegel. "So Mr. McFee, what's this business you have in my Canada."

"I represent a company that contracts for the manufacture of shell casings. We hope we can find —"

The British gentleman interrupted. "Sir, I'm with the British war office. I would advise you to not give away any information. What if someone here were a German ..." Then he glared at the Irishman, "... or had German sympathies. They might pass along your information to someone who would want to know such a thing."

"I hadn't thought of that," Schwegel said. "Sorry."

"You're with the war office? In what capacity?" The Canadian farmer asked.

"For the same reason, I'm going to decline to say." Again, he and the Irish salesman traded glares.

The growing hostility at the table prompted the wives to stand, an announcement that the dinner was finished, and it was time for their husbands to leave as well.

Later, on his way to his cabin, Schwegel saw the British gentleman enter the smoking room. Feeling a dare in it, he decided to follow him in. Several sofas and wing chairs were scattered about the room, which was paneled in dark oak. A pair of white-jacketed waiters moved about, one selling Cuban cigars and Jamaican pipe tobacco and the other taking orders for cognacs and brandies. The seats were quickly filling with men on their way back from dinner. The smoke from pipes and cigars was rapidly filling the room.

The British gentleman, an unlit pipe in hand, took a brandy and settled into a wing chair. Schwegel sat in the one next to it. "Do you mind?"

"Not at all. Have a seat."

"I want to apologize for my slip at dinner. This is my first time going over, and I need to learn some things."

"You caught yourself in time. I make this trip every few months, and you don't know who you're traveling with. That Irishman – his sentiments were clearly with the Germans. I didn't trust him the moment he opened his mouth ... I apologize but when everyone was introduced at dinner, I missed your name. Mine is Kensington."

"McFee."

As Schwegel ordered a brandy from the waiter, Kenginton continued his assault on Irish loyalties. However, Schwegel listened more to how he said these things than what he said. There was something about the British accent he deeply despised – its pompousness, its pretension.

Then Schwegel realized something. They were at war now, he and this gentleman from the British war office. The rules had changed. He could kill this man, if the situation warranted it. Indeed, he was *encouraged* to kill him, and without guilt, if the situation required it.

Schwegel had to smile. War. How wonderful. The license it gave you to do things you would never do in peace – but wanted to.

He sipped his brandy and listened to the man's unrelenting harangue about England's enemies and wondered how he would accomplish the deed, if it were necessary. As with anything else, his mind sought efficiency, simplicity, and speed in the method.

A bullet to the back of his head, he decided.

"Let me ask you," said Kensington. "How are things going in Scotland?"

Schwegel brought his thoughts back to the conversation.

"Good, but we're as worried as you. There's a theory the Germans might invade Scotland first because it would be unexpected, then come down to England from the north."

"We expect everything. We have men in the war office who sit around all day planning for any German strategy you can think of. It's like war college exercises." He tamped his pipe with a silver instrument on his key chain, then lit it. "The worry, though, is that if America doesn't get up its courage and get into this soon, we'll run out of bodies to throw at the fight. Same with the Germans. Both sides are losing men by the thousands every day and gaining no advantage. We need America in this. It would crush the spirt of the Germans if they saw legions of fresh troops coming at them."

"Then how can we get the Americans into it?"

"That's the question, isn't it."

"Your war office friends, they must have a strategy for that."

Pausing a moment, Kensington sent a puff of smoke into the increasingly stale air. "There's a lot of resolve in that country not to fight. Our best hope is that the Germans will sink a few more big liners with Americans on them. If enough innocent women and children go to the bottom, that would convince the Americans."

Seeing the brandy turning the man drowsy, Schwegel decided to wade in a little deeper.

"Your war office friends. I've got some friends who sit around and theorize too. They believe the Americans think they are untouchable where they are, an ocean away. They think if they joined the fight, went over to Europe, and even if Germany won, they could still go home and it would still be America as they knew it."

"Sounds true."

"My friends think that the Germans know this, so to keep America out of it, they will warn them they're not beyond the reach of Germany, of its U-boats and destroyers."

"So you think they'll shell American cities at some point, as a warning?"

"Possibly," Schwegel said.

Kensington shook his head. "It wouldn't be taken as a warning. It would be taken as an act of war. The torn-up bodies of innocent women and children on the sidewalk? You'd have a declaration of war the very next morning." He sent another small cloud of smoke toward the ceiling. "If they want to send a warning to America to keep them out, there's better ways to do it."

"Such as what?"

"Well ... I would have to think about that."

Schwegel did not know if he planned to think

about it at that moment or not. Apparently not, though. The conversation drifted into silence.

The brandy was rapidly doing its work, and Schwegel glanced over to see the man's eyelids fluttering with approaching sleep as he made a last draw on his pipe.

Schwegel watched the smoke cloud melt into the rest of the tobacco haze that lay along the ceiling as a phrase began to play over and over in his mind.

Innocent women and children.

Innocent women and children.

The Marconi room

14

The Telegram

STARTING THE THIRD day out, Schwegel would go down every morning to the Marconi room where the wireless operators sent and received telegrams. Schwegel had been expecting a cable from the Abteilung IIIb man in Halifax about where to meet once the ship landed.

On this morning, one operator was at the magnetic detector. By this time, he recognized Schwegel and motioned to the wire basket on the counter. "You got your message, sir. Please sign the sheet next to it, if you don't mind."

Schwegel sorted through the sealed envelopes in the basket. He stopped at one marked C. J. Kensington. Perhaps it was about war business.

"This one for Kensington. I see him at meals. Can I sign for it too?"

"No, sir. We have strict rules. Just your own."

He debated opening it right there and reading it while

the operator tapped out morse code at the equipment. However, he would have to break the envelope's seal. He left it atop the pile.

In the hallway, he opened his, which contained only two sentences.

Haas will meet you at pier. Will carry green umbrella.

However, walking back to his cabin, it was Kensington's cable he burned to read. He had to smile. He was beginning to embrace his job as a spy, he realized.

Reaching his cabin door, he saw a different steward in the hallway than the one he encountered fifteen minutes earlier. "Excuse me. What time did the overnight man go off?"

"Just a few minutes ago, sir, when the shifts changed. I'll be on the rest of the day. Do you require anything?"

Schwegel shook his head.

In his cabin, he waited a few minutes, put his cable back in its envelope, sealed it with spit, then returned to the Marconi room. A different man, the day man, was now at the equipment and he turned.

"Just checking to see if there's anything in the basket for me," Schwegel said.

He found Kensington's cable, took it, and immediately covered it in his hand with his own.

"Found one. Just sign for it?"

"Please, sir. On the sheet next to it. And please include your cabin number."

Schwegel pretended to sign, hovering the pen over his earlier signature.

In his cabin again, his heart pounding, he unsealed just enough of Kensington's envelope to slip out the folded cable.

Meet Capt. George Wedon – Guest at Palatine Hotel in Halifax – Obtain his machine molds – Return on Concordia sailing March 11 – Carry molds only in personal luggage.

It was signed "Fulbright."

Schwegel memorized the message and tested himself by whispering it out loud several times until he had it word for word. Then he put the telegram back in its envelope, resealing it with spit as much as possible.

Returning to the Marconi room, he slipped Kensington's cable into the basket and grabbed another off the pile in the same motion, all before the operator turned.

"You remember I was in before. But I picked up two envelopes by mistake. Mine and this envelope for Mrs. Bryce. Should I just put hers back?"

The operator came over and examined it. "So you didn't open it?"

"No. You can see it's still sealed. I saw the name right away and realized my mistake."

The operator seemed satisfied. "Then no harm done, sir. I'll put it back. Thanks for your honesty."

Repairing the tracks

15

The Munitions Train

NOLAN, GOING BY the name James O'Connell, met two Secret Service agents and two New York City detectives at the police headquarters in Jersey City. He quickly noticed they treated him like an outsider, like an unwanted guest forced on them. From one comment of a city detective, he took it to be because he was new Irish. ("Do we know if these anarchists are huns or Paddies?") He bristled hearing that slur or any other. Paddy, Mick, spud, coal-cracker, mucker, shant.

The men took a train south to Camden and were picked up by a local sheriff who drove them within a half mile east of the location – to woods the opposite side of the tracks from where the saboteurs were expected to approach. They hiked in with the help of a local fisherman the sheriff knew. A light snow fell as they moved, dusting the frozen forest floor. Once they were in sight of the tracks and Cole Farm Road, they split into three teams and took up different positions on the edge of the forest. A field of low brushy shrubs lay between them and the tracks.

Nolan and a Secret Service agent named Michaels – black thinning hair, eyeglasses, about thirty-five – settled in behind a fallen pitch pine about a hundred yards from the tracks, with the ground beneath them frozen. Their breath was visible in the frigid air. They took turns using their one pair of field glasses to monitor the road.

"So you're Irish." Michaels said.

Nolan tensed up. He knew what would usually follow. "You have an objection to that?"

"Not all all."

"Some men don't want to work with an Irishman what's still got his accent," Nolan said.

"Well, lose it then."

Nolan lowered the glasses and glared at him. "Why don't you lose yours instead, Michaels. I like mine."

Michaels raised his hands and smiled. "Don't get upset. I was joking."

"I doubt it. What you meant is 'stop sounding like a damned Mick so I can stand working with you.'"

"I'd never say something like that."

"People don't say it. They think it. That's how being Irish in this country is."

"I apologize if it came out wrong. Honestly, I'd never say that to hurt someone."

They grew silent and watched the road with Michaels taking the glasses. It was twenty minutes to ten o'clock. Despite wearing gloves and earmuffs, Nolan felt his hands and ears starting to lose sensation in the freezing air.

"I heard you're working undercover," Michaels said.

"I heard you're trying to get into the German groups behind these bombings. Learn anything yet?"

"I'm not allowed to talk about it."

"Here's a story for you, O'Connell. When I started with the Department of the Treasury, for the first six months, I worked undercover in Buffalo. A secret anti-Catholic organization up there was burning down churches but also counterfeiting money. So I worked my way into the group. I said I was Presbyterian and hated the Catholics. Why I'm telling you this is not to give you advice on how to work undercover. I've found there's no advice that's any good. You have to figure it out yourself as you go. Why I'm telling you is this." Michaels lowered the glasses and looked at Nolan as if what was to follow was going to be important. "My name wasn't originally Michaels. It was Mickelberg. It's Jewish. Some people hate Jews worse than the Irish or the Catholics."

Surprised by the confession, Nolan turned. "So you changed your name?"

"My parents did when I was a baby and they first came to America. But this group in Buffalo, if they found out I was Jewish, well, you can imagine. I used to have to listen to their hateful venom and keep quiet. It almost gave me an ulcer."

"Maybe there were Jews in the group. I know with the Irish, there are some who can hate with the best of them."

"Maybe. But I want to say something to you. What I learned from that situation is that you're only yourself and you have to make your own rules about how to treat other people. You're not an American, an Irishman, a Jew, a Catholic, a Democrat, a Republican, you're not anything. You're just yourself. You're a country all alone in the world and you have to write your own rules about everything. You have to write your own Constitution, your own Bill of Rights."

They were quiet. Nolan respected what he had said. He knew this was one of the deeply felt lessons some people reached in life and he respected that Michaels was someone who valued deeply felt lessons. However, he himself had not yet completely reached that particular lesson. He was still Irish.

"Let me ask you, Michaels. You look English so that's what people probably think. Right? When they ask your religion, what do you answer?"

"I don't. If I have to, I say I'm Presbyterian."

"Now, see? Saying you're something you're not, Presbyterian, I don't agree with that. I might lose my accent little by little, but if people ask me where I'm from, I'll always say Ireland."

Michaels laughed. "I wouldn't mind being Irish. You people are such proud bastards."

"Change your name to McMichael. I'll teach you how to roll your R's. And cocky – that's the main thing. Learn to be cocky."

"Maybe I could teach you to be Jewish."

"I thought you said Presbyterian."

"I still go to synagogues sometimes, if I feel troubled."

Nolan smiled. "Good for you, Mickelberg." He took the glasses and watched the road.

"One thing," Michaels said. "Don't tell anyone anything I just told you. These men I work with don't know I'm Jewish. Life is easier if they don't. All right?"

Nolan nodded agreement. Within a minute, he saw

the smoke of a motor on Cole Farm Road. "Looks like they're here."

The plan was to let the men do their job sabotaging the tracks, but to let them leave before moving in. That way, they would believe Nolan was on their side, giving him admittance to their spy ring.

Michaels traded hand signals with the two other teams. Everyone stayed in place as they continued to watch a roadster pull up to the tracks. Two men got out of the motor and took a device the size of a shoebox from the back seat. Then they struggled to dig a hole in the frozen gravel beneath one of the parallel rails and carefully placed the package in the crevice. One lit a match and lowered it to the device. They stood for a moment and admired their work. Then they got back in the roadster and left, the smoking engine marking their progress along the road as they exited.

"What now?" Nolan asked.

"We've got a man from the bomb squad. That's him running toward the tracks."

Nolan watched through the glasses as the agent sprinted through the woods then out into a snow dusted field of low brush. When he came to the tracks and the device, he studied the bomb with his field glasses from about thirty yards away before carefully approaching it. Crouching, he examined it for only a few seconds before he motioned with great waves of his arms for the other teams to come in.

"This thing never would have blown," the agent said as they all arrived. "The fools didn't set a proper fuse. It went out in the cold anyway."

He ripped the device from beneath the rail, removed

two of the three dynamite sticks and, using a penknife, cut the fuse and reattached it to one of the sticks. Then he motioned to everyone to back up. They did. He put the stick back under the rail where it joined with another, lit the fuse and ran.

The explosion was enough to break the rails apart at the joint plate, twisting the rail ends. They all moved in to see it.

"They're mangled enough that it looks like these idiots did their job," said the bomb squad agent.

Another agent had brought a camera with him and photographs were taken. As he was doing this, a train approached so slowly from the south that Nolan did not hear it until it had nearly reached them. A locomotive and two freight cars. Three Secret Service agents climbed out of the front freight car as did a team of a half dozen trainmen who carried a new steel rail and tools.

Within fifteen minutes, the mangled rail was changed out for the new one, the joint plate and tie spikes were hammered in place, the gravel bed was raked smooth, and more photographs were taken.

"This'll be in every paper in New York tomorrow morning," the bomb squad agent said. "So good work gentlemen."

Before they started the hike out, Michaels gave Nolan a folded slip of paper. "Undercover work is hard," he said. "If you hit a problem, you can call me at that number."

— ❊ —

Nolan saw the story, with three photographs, in the *Herald* before breakfast.

MUNITIONS DISASTER AVERTED

Saboteurs try to derail du Pont train

Saboteurs were nearly successful yesterday in derailing a train bound for the Jersey City piers carrying explosive powder that was to be shipped overseas for the Allied cause.

While the saboteur's incendiary device managed to sever the rail line as it passed through southern New Jersey, a sharp-eyed guard on the munitions train spotted the break ahead and halted the train before the derailment could occur.

"Had the train been traveling with any speed as it came to the break, it might have crashed and exploded. We were very fortunate," said R. Thomas Meeks, a spokesman for the Pennsylvania Railroad.

Henrik Baumann leads the church meeting

16

Secret Cell

THE MEETING WAS in the empty basement assembly room of Holy Cross Church on West 42nd Street on a Saturday morning. As Nolan walked in, Baumann, O'Keefe, and several men Nolan did not know were there. They sat around a coal stove, passing a flask of whiskey among them. The Bibles that had been on the chairs were in a stack on the floor.

Nolan noticed that none had German accents, not even Baumann. He wondered if that was a deliberate strategy of the ring, to recruit men who did not sound German – Irishmen and American-born men of German ancestry – to make detection less likely.

"Shake the hand of James O'Connell," Baumann said to the group. "A good friend that's already done good work for us. The train bombing in New Jersey yesterday – James set that up for us. Not his fault it didn't go as expected, but good work anyway. What we're discussing is the situation last night."

"What situation is that?" Nolan asked.

"You ain't heard?" O'Keefe said. "Up in the Bronx. Some of our boys is got a house on Fulton Avenue and it blew up. The whole second floor. One of them survived it, Mooney, and he's telling police it was a package what got delivered that exploded when they opened it ... But it weren't."

The story told by O'Keefe, who visited Mooney in the hospital just an hour earlier, was that they were making a five-stick bomb in a nail keg and it went off. The head of one man landed on the roof of a garage next door, the arm of another lodged in the mudguard of a Dodge motor parked across the street.

Then the talk turned to the need for a public funeral.

"They were all Irish Catholic heroes," O'Keefe said. "So a Catholic Mass and a procession up Eighth Avenue. I was thinking next Saturday morning."

"You have to have it by Wednesday," Baumann said. "The law is that the bodies can only be held for four days at the morgue, then they go to Fresh Pond."

"What's Fresh Pond?" Nolan asked.

"It's where the city crematorium is," Baumann said. "The bodies are at the morgue at Fordham Hospital right now. You either have to have the funeral by Wednesday or get a court order to hold them in the morgue."

"No judge'll give a court order for anarchists to get paraded through the streets," said a man named Schmidt.

"Then the procession has to be Wednesday," O'Keefe said.

"No. Tuesday," Baumann said. "You counted wrong. The explosion was last night. Count it. Today's Saturday, that's one, Sunday, Monday, Tuesday."

"You ain't gonna get a crowd on such short notice on a Tuesday, a work day. Then it'll look like no one cares these heroes died," O'Keefe said. "That's worse than no funeral."

It was agreed. Let the bodies go to Fresh Pond.

"What about the list?" Schmidt asked. "How do we find out if the police found it?"

"What list?" Nolan asked.

"Mooney told me they had made up a wish list for the bombing day, people they wanted to blow up like Morgan and Rockefeller," O'Keefe said.

"What bombing day?" Nolan asked, trying to seem innocent about it.

Baumann leaned in confidentially. "Something's coming soon, something big, but we can't tell you about it. In fact, we don't really know all about it. That's for the men higher up. All we know is it will be bigger than anything we've done before."

"Can I help? If it's big, you must need men to help."

"You can stand ready. We'll tell you if they need another hand."

Nolan smiled as if trying to make light of it. "So you're telling me we four are not the higher ups."

Baumann smiled. "I wish, but no. There's higher ups then there are higher ups above them. That's how a good organization works. O'Keefe and I keep in touch with the ones above us and they have a man that does the same with the men above them."

O'Keefe said there was an Irish patrolman out of the Highbridge Station in the Bronx who could check to see if the list had been found by police in the wrecked home.

"He's a friend to us. I'll see if I can reach him after we're done. He's on duty today I think."

The rest of the meeting was to plan a surveillance trip to the new Remington Cartridge Factory in Bridgeport, Connecticut, to determine if there was a way to break in to set bombs.

"All it's in business for is to make bullets for the British. Why don't O'Connell and I go," said O'Keefe. "I got a cousin in Bridgeport we could stay with tonight."

Nolan planned to be home with Sheenagh this night, but he tried to show no objection.

It was agreed. The two of them would go that afternoon. There was talk of what to look for, positions of guard towers, the strength of fences and so forth.

"Go home and get lunch," O'Keefe told him. "We'll meet at Grand Central by the information stand at two. I'll have the train tickets."

Checking tickets

17

Trip to Bridgeport

O'KEEFE WAS WAITING by the information booth in the main concourse of Grand Central Terminal, a cavernous room with a vaulted ceiling that featured the constellations of the night sky.

When he saw Nolan approaching, he waved the tickets in the air. "We gotta hurry. Train's about to leave."

They rushed down a flight of stairs to the platform where passengers were already boarding.

Settling into a seat in a largely empty rear car, Nolan noticed for the first time how shabbily O'Keefe was dressed. Stained blue denim overalls, a rumpled flannel shirt, a peaked hat, and leather boots. He asked him why.

"We want to look like machinists," O'Keefe said, "like we're set for a shift making bullets. You didn't have anything to wear worse than that?"

Nolan had worn his everyday wool suit and derby. "I'll just say I'm a firearm salesman."

Several more people boarded the car, looked at

O'Keefe with some disdain, then kept walking to the next car. Nolan noticed how well dressed the men were, like bankers and lawyers.

Once the train jerked away from the station, the conductor arrived to take tickets. O'Keefe handed him the paper slips. Nolan noticed the suspicious look the conductor gave them.

"You know you're on an express limited," the conductor said.

"You don't think I can afford it?" O'Keefe remarked.

"I just wanted to point it out to you."

"Consider it pointed out."

The conductor moved on and O'Keefe gestured his contempt, flicking his fingers beneath his chin, something another passenger saw.

"This ain't a local, which is what poor bastards like us usually ride. I guess he thinks we made a mistake, getting on a limited. But there's a lot of money being spread around by the Germans so why not spend some of it."

O'Keefe said the German government was spending tens of thousands of dollars in America to back labor strikes at plants involved in munitions, shipbuilding, or any other war work that benefitted the Allies. "And what we do is getting its share also. So you and I, when we travel, it's on the best trains. This one's got a first-class dining car, if you get hungry."

They were out of the tunnels beneath the city, rattling north along the rail lines through the Bronx. It was early March, windy and cold. A dirty layer of snow, bereft of any of the charm it had when it fell weeks earlier, blanketed the city. This only made the ugliness of the homes and businesses that resided by the tracks worse – tenements, motor repair shops, industrial warehouses.

Nolan retrieved an abandoned *Herald* wedged in the seat cushions across the aisle and began to read it. "POPE CALLS WAR THE SUICIDE OF EUROPE." "GERMAN SHELLS FALL ON VERDUN." "ZEPPELINS RAID ENGLISH COAST."

Over the newspaper, he could see O'Keefe fidgeting in his seat. Nolan's impression was that O'Keefe brought him along to be his audience. The new man sitting at the feet of the veteran. He guessed O'Keefe was upset that he was not paying him enough attention. He put down the newspaper.

O'Keefe stopped fidgeting. "I don't know if you understand who you've fallen in with," O'Keefe said. He turned to make sure no other passenger was near enough to hear. "But I was one of the men who set that fire at the Roebling Plant in Trenton last year. They make the wire netting that traps U-boats."

"Is that right? You were back of that? What else have you done?"

"A lot of things. I shouldn't say, though."

"Let me ask. How big is this group?"

"How big is what group?"

"This group I've fallen in with. Is it just a dozen or so men?"

O'Keefe stared at him like he was crazy. "A dozen? More like forty or fifty. It's organized. Like layers of an onion is what they always say, circles inside circles."

"Where are we? An outside layer? Or inside?"

"We're not the center but close. Baumann is someone important. He goes in to the German Consulate every week and talks to someone there."

"The center of the organization – who is that?"

"On this big job coming up, it's the German who's coming."

"A German?"

"A specialist in explosives. It's someone especially trained for the big bombings what's coming up."

"You said bombings. So there are many planned?"

"All on one day is what I hear. You'll hear about it soon enough."

Nolan had the feeling he was pushing this braggart to a point that he might notice he was being pushed, so he stopped asking questions.

"Don't worry, though," O'Keefe said. "You won't be asked to do nothing you don't want to do. One time, Baumann wanted me to kill someone's mistress to send him a message. I said I wouldn't kill no women unless it's a bomb that did it indirectly because they were in the wrong place at the wrong time. Baumann understood. He did it himself."

Appearing satisfied that sufficient attention had been paid him, O'Keefe grew silent, gazing out the window at the passing landscape. Nolan was able to go back to the *Herald*.

Soon they were in Connecticut, and after a stop in Stamford, the conductor came to the door. "Bridgeport next stop! Bridgeport in twenty-eight minutes!"

A passenger at the far end rose to say something to the conductor and Nolan saw the conductor glance in their direction before he left the car.

A half hour later, signs for Bridgeport businesses began passing their window, then Nolan saw the station approaching. However, the train came to a stop far short of the platform.

The conductor came to the door. "There will be a slight delay in disembarking. Please keep your seats."

Nolan could see ahead on the platform where another conductor from a front car exited the train and spoke to a baggage handler who went inside the station. In a moment, a police officer came out to talk to the conductor.

"We need to get off right now. Something's wrong," Nolan said.

"Stop worrying. Just wait here. There's delays like this all the time."

The conductor and the officer climbed down off the platform and began walking on the gravel bed toward the train, with the officer drawing his revolver.

"No, get off! Right now, O'Keefe. Now!" Nolan rose and walked rapidly to the rear of the car. He glanced back to see that O'Keefe had not budged, an expression of arrogant disinterest on his face.

The car's doors were electrically locked, but an emergency handle allowed him to force open the door on the side away from the approaching officer. He dropped down into the gravel and then began running up the tracks, away from the train, until an opening in the fence allowed him to escape into the back yards of surrounding tenements and industrial buildings. He never looked back.

He walked for nearly an hour, his fingers and ears gradually numbing in the freezing temperatures and icy wind. Eventually, he reached a trolley line on the edge of Fairfield. From there, he traveled to the Fairfield train station and was able to board a local back to Grand Central.

He finally reached home in Brooklyn at nearly midnight, cold, hungry, exhausted, and miserable. He found their spare key hidden behind a loose board in the hallway wainscoting and went in. The apartment was darkened. He stood at the bedroom door and could heard Sheenagh's light breathing as she slept. As quietly as he could, he undressed in the bathroom with the lights off, amid the rich lavender aroma of her bath soap. Then he crept across the bedroom floor and slipped beneath the warm sheets with her. She woke briefly, just enough to whisper his name, before her eyes closed again.

This would be the reward, he told himself as sleep began to overcome him. Finish this assignment, find this German, then go back to accounting. Never again miss any nights in this bed.

Woodside train yard

18

The Higher Ups

ON MONDAY MORNING, Tunney's cousin assigned Nolan permanently to a section of tracks being improved in Woodside, just over the Queensborough Bridge on Long Island. He did it so they would never have to talk to or see each other again.

Nolan got to the Woodside yard before nine o'clock and had to shake his head in despair. To each side of the tracks were trash heaps resembling those you saw from trains rolling by the Harlem swamps.

Trains barreled through the Woodside yard on their way to or from Manhattan. However, the yard also collected the refuse of the neighborhood as well as broken and discarded furniture and other detritus – three-legged chairs, wheelless baby carriages, shattered window panes. And now, on one of the warmer days of late winter, the yard reeked of a winter's worth of thawing garbage.

Nolan found the yardmaster in his shed.

"I'm here to pull up ties," Nolan said. "Tunney sent

me. I'm O'Connell."

The man checked a sheet. "Says here you come when you want. That's a fine job."

Nolan looked out over the yard. "Doesn't look like it to me."

"Just report to me when you get here, report out when you leave. A half hour for lunch. Pick up your crowbar from me, drop it with me when you leave. It's right there by the door."

Feeling like he had been relegated to some part of hell, he put on his work gloves and picked up the bar on his way out the door.

Tunney had told him one set of tracks on a siding through the yard was gradually being replaced by tracks nearby that sat atop a new type of tie, soaked in creosote to last longer. While a small crew worked to install the new tracks, his job was to dig the old, untreated ties, about a hundred yards worth of them, out of the partially frozen track bed and stack them.

The work, he quickly found, was back-breaking, the conditions unbearable.

— ⊰❖⊱ —

"O'Connell. Are you in there?" The knocking was insistent.

"Just a second." Nolan, still in his work clothes, was in his bedroom in his Hell's Kitchen apartment, washing a wound on his ankle produced by the jagged edge of something he accidentally encountered at the yard earlier in the day.

He rolled down his pants leg and went to the door. It was Henrik Baumann.

"What happened in Bridgeport Saturday?" Irritated,

Baumann came in and closed the door behind him.

"O'Keefe didn't tell you?"

"O'Keefe's in jail."

Exhausted, his ankle throbbing in pain, Nolan told the story as he finished washing and bandaging the wound in the kitchen. The ride on the limited, the suspicious conductor, the train stopping outside the station, the police officer pulling his gun, O'Keefe refusing to get off, his own flight to Fairfield.

"Why's O'Keefe in jail?" Nolan asked.

"He resisted arrest and he stumbled telling his story. He told one thing to one officer, something else to another. So O'Keefe is finished with us for the moment."

"O'Keefe is an idiot, to tell you the truth." Nolan said with spontaneous honesty, in part out of exhaustion.

Baumann laughed out loud. "You're absolutely right. O'Keefe *is* an idiot. I knew that, but he did what we asked him to do ... That cut – did you get that running from the station?"

"No, working. I had to put in a day on the tracks today. I still have to earn a living, a miserable living."

For a moment, Baumann watched him apply the linen bandage. "Maybe we can help you with that, O'Connell, give you a salary so you can quit your job. What would you say about that?"

Nolan could again reply with honesty. "I'd like that a lot."

"We'll have to get you a new identity too," he said. He continued to study Nolan as he finished dressing the wound. "You know, there's something smart about you. You knew there was going to be a problem at that station and you took action to get off that train. You can think clearly in the middle of trouble. We need that. Why don't you eat your dinner, and I'll be back in a couple of hours. There's a meeting tonight I want you to attend with me."

———❦———

As they parked in an alley behind a grocery warehouse on 35th Street near the docks, Baumann told him who would be there. "These are the men above me, the planners. I just want you to keep quiet. I'll introduce you as O'Keefe's replacement. He was the second man in our group and the one these men would contact if they couldn't get hold of me. Now that's you."

The meeting was in an empty cold storage locker on the warehouse's second floor. Chairs had been set out in a circle. There were puddles from the melted ice in the corners, and one half-filled crate of wilted lettuce lay by a wall, giving the room a stale stink.

Six men, including Baumann and Nolan, took the seats. The heavy oak door was shut by a guard standing just outside.

There were no introductions except of James O'Connell, which Baumann made. "He set up that bombing of the du Pont train in New Jersey for us. I had my boys shadow him for several days in the rail yards and our man in the records office in Boston, where he worked before New York, checked him out also, so I trust him. He's going to be the new second contact man for our group."

That sent a shiver of fear through Nolan. He had not been aware of any of this. What if they followed him home to Brooklyn some night?

"Mr. O'Connell," said the oldest of the men who, with his paternal manner, white hair, and beard, Nolan took to be head of this group. His accent was German but his English was refined. "What we're going to be doing might result in the deaths of many people. Is that something that will concern you?"

"Of course it will."

They all looked at him with mild shock. Even Nolan was surprised he had said it.

"It should concern every man in this room," he quickly said, trying to recover. "But what I mean is that, well, what we do has to be important enough to justify these deaths. That's the point of war, isn't it? You take lives to save lives."

Several of the men nodded. "Wise." "Splendid." "Well said."

From that point on, the group ignored Nolan out of an acceptance of him. He was silent as they talked, thinking instead. He was astonished he had said what he said to recover, but at the same time, he realized it was exactly the thing he needed to say to win their confidence. He had acted out of instincts that he was surprised he even had.

As he listened, he noticed some in this group had German accents. A man named Voigt and another. The true Germans, he thought.

He hoped details of the bombings would be mentioned, but few were. The conversation mainly centered around the need to finance labor strikes on the docks and in the munitions plants.

When it did turn to the bombings, only one detail of importance emerged. The group leader was asked by Baumann about the progress of the bombing plot.

"I have one bit of information," the leader responded. "The German will soon land and be in New York City a week or so after that. We'll know more then."

"What German?" Nolan asked, trying to make the question seem like innocent curiosity.

"A man is being sent, an explosives specialist," the leader said. "That's all you need to know."

"You need to know more than that about someone you're trusting your life with," another man said.

There was grumbling among the others.

"Don't form judgments yet," the leader counseled them. "Let's just wait to meet him."

"I've heard he's very young," Schmidt said. "Vat does he know? And to put him in charge – dat's ridiculous."

"Conrad, you proposed this mission. You know the targets. Why is someone else being brought in to lead it? Sounds stupid."

There were mumbled affirmations of this.

The leader, Conrad apparently, smiled at the vote of confidence in his leadership. "As I said, my friends, no judgments yet. Wait."

The discussion moved back to the labor strikes.

A half hour later, as the meeting showed signs of coming to an end, Nolan felt a boldness and spoke up. "Can I ask what I can do to help?"

Baumann put his hand on Nolan's arm to restrain him, but Conrad seemed pleased with his eagerness. "Just listen to Henrik. He'll tell you what you need to know."

"Can I ask what you will be bombing? Are there railroad targets I can help you with?"

To this, Conrad seemed less pleased, as if Nolan were pushing too hard. "Not railroads, but we'll let you know eventually."

Instinctively, Nolan knew to ask nothing more. He

nodded and tried to seem like the eager new recruit, anx-
ious to do a good job, perhaps over-anxious, but with
good intentions. They seemed to take it as that.

Driving back uptown in Baumann's motor, though,
Nolan got more information than he had from the
meeting.

"I've heard they're making forty bombs timed to go off
all at the same moment," Baumann said. "We've already
got a watchmaker making the timers and shipping them
to us one by one. And we've got a manufacturer in
Connecticut who's been making numerous small purchases of sulfuric acid and nitric acid and storing it for us.
You put them together to make TNT. By God, it'll be like
the Fourth of July when all these bombs go off."

"When do they go off? Is it the Fourth of July?"

"Well before that, but wouldn't that have been funny if
it was. You don't need to know the date right now,
though."

"Can I ask who's this man who's coming, this
German?"

"You don't need to know that either."

At the dock in Halifax

19

The *Bristol Star* Lands

THE GREEN UMBRELLA stood out out even on the pier crowded with people there to meet the *Bristol Star*. Schwegel, pulling his own trunk, was in the first wave of passengers to disembark in a light drizzle, moving slowly down the gangplank behind four elderly passengers being pushed in wheelchairs by stewards.

"Are you Haas?"

"Are you McFee?"

They shook hands. Haas, about forty, his hair slicked back, a diamond stickpin in his tie, immediately struck Schwegel as wealthy although the clothes by themselves were not enough to create the impression. What was there about him that did?

Schwegel puzzled it out as Haas walked off to hail a taxicab. Perhaps it was the youthfulness in his face. Haas had to be past forty, but around his eyes, he looked twenty. Rich men often aged slower in the face, Schwegel had observed. The weight of years toiling in a hateful job gave the poor man bitter lines around his eyes and mouth by the time he was forty. A rich man could escape that.

They took a taxi to the Victoria Hotel but only talked about the weather at sea and in Halifax, as they rode. However, once on the sidewalk outside the hotel, Schwegel excitedly told him about the cable he had intercepted.

"Molds. What kind of molds?"

"I imagine molds to make parts of something," Schwegel said.

"If this man was from the British War Office and they sent him personally to Halifax to get them, then they're important," Haas said. "Let me look into it. Why don't you go up to my room, get a meal if you want, and …" He looked his pocket watch. "… it's one fifteen. I'll meet you back here at six. We'll have some dinner and then get on the road."

"On the road where?"

"To the United States," he said, handing Schwegel his key. "You'll be at the Maine border by midnight tomorrow."

⁕

Absent the rolling motion of the *Bristol Star*, Schwegel fell into a deep sleep soon after he stretched out on Haas' bed. He woke only when a porter knocked repeatedly on the hotel door.

"What?"

"Sir. I have a message for you. It's from Mr. Haas. I'll slip it under the door."

Groggily, Schwegel retrieved the envelope lying on the carpet and opened it.

Can't meet you for dinner. Will

**meet you at eight in the lobby. Be
ready to travel. Try the ribs of beef
in horseradish in the dining room.**

At eight o'clock, refreshed by the sleep, a bath, and the dinner, he was in the lobby with his trunk when Haas returned.

"Let me go upstairs and get my things, then we'll get off," Haas said.

Haas' motor, parked in the hotel driveway, was a gleaming new Packard Twin Six touring car. Indeed, he had to be wealthy.

They motored out of Halifax in the dark, the road illuminated only by the auto's huge headlamps and a three-quarter moon.

Haas, Schwegel quickly learned, was an Austrian and the nephew of the Grand Duke of Mecklenburg-Strelitz. Judging by his constant joking references to the war, this was an adventure for him. Schwegel instantly felt they were kindred spirits.

"I almost forgot," Schwegel said. "What about the Brit and the molds? Find out anything on that?"

"It's taken care of. That's why I was late. A confederate and I managed to get into their room at the Palatine Hotel."

"Did you find the molds?"

"Yes, we did and they're on their way to Germany. Very good work, McFee. They were molds for machine gun parts. And we got the design too. It's a new type that shoots five hundred rounds per minute and is water cooled. So very good work, my friend."

"Then the Brit will be going back to England empty-handed and humiliated."

"He won't be going back. Neither will his friend. But that's not your concern." Then Haas smiled. "While we were in the room, they came back from dinner. I won't say what followed, but we had to strangle them and after they were dead, we undressed them and put them in bed together naked and put their hands around each other's throats. Let the British War Office chew on that."

Schwegel laughed at the irony.

As the road out of Halifax turned from pavement to packed dirt and became more difficult to drive, their conversation faded and he had a chance to consider what he had done. He could see Kensington, his face relaxed by brandy, across from him in the smoking room that night at sea. And now he was dead, killed, indirectly, by Schwegel.

He drew back on his own thoughts, attempting to assess how he felt at that moment. He had killed this man as certainly as if he had strangled him himself, the first time in his life a death had been his responsibility. How did that make him feel? He waited for any emotion about it to identify itself. However, none did at first. If anything, he felt a calm coldness. Men died in war and he might die and tens of thousands had already died and that was the truth and reality of war. It was not his concern – only the mission was.

However, as the Packard traveled on into the night, Schwegel began to feel a growing exhilaration. This was why he wanted this war, he realized – to have these types of things happen, experiences that involved death, experiences that would tell him more about life and reality than anything else that would ever happen to him.

Just after midnight, they pulled into the dirt drive of a
dairy farm outside Moncton, still four hours from the
Canadian border with Maine. Carl Mueller, a widower of
German ancestry, owned the forty-acre farm. He was
also a member of the New Brunswick Provincial
Legislature.

Mueller and Haas seemed to be old friends, Schwegel
observed.

"I have thirty-one cows, but my government wants me
to get rid of them and breed horses and mules," said
Mueller, white-haired, perhaps in his sixties. "The army
needs them for the war. I told them I will not create an
animal that will only get blown to pieces. I tell them it's
cruel."

"That's very noble," Schwegel said.

"That's not the reason, though. This captain who asks
me to produce these animals, he thinks I am Pennsylvania
Dutch originally, which is true. So he thinks, ah, you are
American and so you must have British sympathies. But
he is stupid. We were German before Pennsylvania. So
we are German first. I will not breed animals to help the
British."

Haas, who had missed dinner, asked for a plate and
Mueller led them to the kitchen as he continued railing
against the British. Schwegel at first thought the man's
ranting was amusing. An old man getting excited like that
– it showed spirit. However, as it went on and became
more angry and vicious, it seemed to have more to do
with Mueller than the issues of the war.

Afterward, Mueller led them upstairs to their rooms.
Haas was given the guest room and Schwegel was taken

to his son's room farther down the hall.

When Schwegel asked Mueller where his son was, the man grumbled, "Don't let it bother you. I'll just say he's not here, so it's not your concern. Let's just say he defied me and unfortunately he paid a price."

This was so provocative that, after Mueller went back downstairs, Nolan went to Haas' room.

"Mueller's son. What happened to him?"

"First, let me show you this." Haas opened his suitcase and took out something wrapped in newspaper. He drew a pistol from it. "This is a Webley self-loading model. It's yours. And this is a Maxim silencer fitted for this pistol. You just screw it onto the barrel like this. See? Simple. Tomorrow, before we go back on the road, you'll have a chance to shoot targets with it."

Schwegel handled the pistol for a moment, hefting it for weight and balance, admiring the workmanship. "But tell me, what about the son?"

Haas closed the bedroom door first. "Many years ago, when he was twelve, Mueller's son broke a lamp while running in the house against his father's rules. Apparently, he broke his rules repeatedly, always angering his father. Mueller beat him and the boy died of a hemorrhage. Mueller refused to believe it was serious and didn't take him to the hospital. A year later, his wife died of a broken heart. Now Mueller is alone with his cows."

"He probably thinks it served the son right. I think it served Mueller right."

"That's so often the way life is," Haas said. "Maybe people get what they deserve even when they don't believe they deserve any such thing."

The two men looked at each other and laughed at the

unexpected truth of the statement. Then their gazes turned back to the pistol in Schwegel's hand as he pointed it at different objects around the bedroom, closing one eye to sight along the barrel.

———⋙———

The handkerchief was pinned to a fence post on the edge of a pasture about thirty yards away. The morning was warm enough that patches of vegetation had pushed through the little remaining snow.

Schwegel, with a box of bullets at his feet, held the Webley, with its silencer on the barrel, at arms length and squeezed the trigger. A mild thudding sound issued from the pistol. However, the handkerchief did not move. Only a breeze a moment later managed to cause it to flutter at all.

He squinted and fired again. This time, a splinter of wood came flying off the edge of the ancient fence post. Better, he told himself. However, it took a reloading and another four shots before the handkerchief showed a blackened hole.

As he reloaded again, Schwegel spotted a crow land just in front of the fence to pick at the emerging vegetation. He hurriedly raised the pistol and fired at it. He missed and the bird seemed only slightly disconcerted by the spray of snow that flew up a yard away. Schwegel fired again and this time the hit came only a foot from the crow, close enough for it to realize it was time to leave.

Schwegel smiled. He looked about the field. Here and there, other birds could be seen landing to forage. He recognized some as similar to those seen in Europe, mainly starlings and sparrows.

Schwegel moved to the fence, crouching behind it to

use it as a shooting blind. Then he waited for a bird to land in the pasture beyond. A bold little black and white bird, looking like an English willow tit, did land on a fence post just ten yards from him, hopping on the post top to see what it could see in different directions. Schwegel aimed carefully and fired. The bird flew off as if punched from its perch, some loose feathers fluttering about in the trail it took in the air.

Schwegel stood and laughed out loud with delight, then he turned to see if Haas may have been watching from the house. He was not.

He reloaded and walked slowly about the yard, looking for more birds, stalking prey.

By the time the box of bullets was empty, he had killed five starlings and wounded a crow badly enough that its struggling, uneven flight of escape meant it would not survive.

Robert Fay's arrest photo

20

German Spies

"**S**HEENAGH, DON'T GET out of bed just yet. Please."

"It's nearly eight o'clock."

"There's no rule that says eight." He playfully pulled her back toward him and wrapped her in his arms.

"Aren't you hungry, though?"

"I can eat anytime … Have you been staying upstairs with the Shapiros?"

"Yes, but it's awkward. You know she lost her baby two months ago. They had a room ready for it and she bought clothes and toys. It's so sad. They put out a cot by the empty crib and I sleep on that."

"Why don't we buy the crib from them so she won't have to see it?"

"No," Sheenagh said. "She wants a baby so bad. The crib is good for her. It gives her hope … I'm not sure I want to ask this, but how has your detective work been? Is it dangerous?"

He knew to lie to her, to spare her the worry. "Not at all. I just attend meetings and write down what I hear in the neighborhood." He lightly put his hand on her stomach. "Do you feel anything yet?"

"Kicking? No."

"Can I listen?" She nodded and he put his ear on her nightgown over the small swell.

"What do you expect to hear?" She asked.

"Dada. Mama. Let me out of here."

"Seriously, do you hear a heartbeat?"

He listened carefully. "Hard to say."

"Well, if it's growling you hear it's because I'm hungry. I'm getting up, John." She rolled out of bed and this time he let her go. She turned at the door. "By the way, I've been cutting out all the newspaper articles that mention spies and such, like you asked. There are several in the envelope on the night table."

Staying in bed, he reached over for them. The most recent was from yesterday's morning *Telegram*, a story about German sabotage plots in New York City.

The story had photographs of Franz von Papen, the former military attache to the German Embassy in Washington who had run a spy ring centered in New York, and Robert Fay, a German national who had been leading the mission to destroy freighters in New York harbor, ships that were loaded with munitions bound for the Allies. Fay planned to use an ingenious bomb that would attach to the rudder posts on the hulls of the ships.

Von Papen was expelled from the country. Fay was awaiting trial.

Nolan had seen the arrest photo of a defiant Fay numerous times in newspapers. What struck him was the man's soulless stare. It was this image Nolan conjured whenever he thought of this new explosives expert coming to New York.

He would walk the streets of the city assessing every face he passed, looking for something, a subtle sneer, a coldness in the eyes, that would say that this, perhaps, was the new German specialist. He knew it was foolish, but it had become almost instinctive, this desire to find the man in the sea of faces.

Secret Service agent Roger Adcock

21

The Meeting

C APTAIN TUNNEY'S OFFICE was on the second
floor at police headquarters in lower Manhattan.
Suspecting the building might be watched by the
Germans, Nolan travelled downtown wearing a disguise
of eyeglasses and a theatrical wig that Tunney got him
from the confiscated property room at police headquarters. He took a circuitous route to evade anyone following
him.

However, at headquarters, the desk sergeant refused to
let him up the stairs, so Tunney had to come down.

"Let this man up any time he comes in," Tunney said.

"Is this what he'll be wearing every time?"

"John, take off the wig and glasses and let him see
what you look like?"

"Captain, should I?"

Tunney thought a moment. "No. You're right.
Sergeant, if he comes in, just call me in my office."

"How do I know it's him what's standing here if he's

disguised every time?"

Tunney sighed with exasperation. "Anyone looking this strange comes in looking for me, call me in my office before you arrest him."

The meeting only involved Tunney, Nolan, and a Secret Service agent sent up from Washington especially for this investigation, Roger Adcock. Round-faced, balding, and well dressed, he had a smugness about him, an air of Washington self-importance.

The Secret Service, which was part of the Department of the Treasury, began to seriously investigate German spy rings after the sinking of the *Lusitania* in May 1915.

They met in a small administrative conference room down the hall from Tunney's office. Dark oak paneling, a polished black table, a half dozen chairs, a framed map of Manhattan as well as photographs of the recent mayors and police commissioners on the wall.

As Nolan took off his disguise, Adcock eyed him with suspicion.

"This one of your men, Tunney?"

"No. I brought him in special."

"From what department?"

"No department. It's not your concern. Let's get this started. I have a meeting in —"

"I have to know who I'm talking to. Where's his file? What does the Secret Service know about him?"

Exasperated, Tunney sighed again. "Not now, Adcock. I want to start."

Adcock narrowed his eyes and drew himself up in his chair. "Excuse me?"

Hearing a challenge in Adcock's voice, Tunney looked

up and was silent, apparently waiting for Adcock to make his intent clear.

"I want to know who this man is," Adcock said.

"It's none of your business for the purposes of this meeting. I know who he is and I know who you are, and that's the way it's going to stay."

Adcock stood and glared at Tunney, then at Nolan. "What's your name?"

"The name I'm using or my actual name?"

"What's your damn name, man?"

"He's not going to tell you," Tunney said with a flash of anger. "And I'm not going to tell you either. Sit the hell down, and for the last time, let's get this going."

Adcock did not sit down. "You want me to confide details of the Secret Service's investigation with a … a damned Irishman I don't know the first thing about? Not a chance, Tunney."

Now Tunney angrily stood, but before he could respond, Adcock, gesturing with a sweeping wave of his arm, said. "And I don't know who you think the Secret Service is, which I'm here in New York representing, but we are an agency invested with the responsibility to keep this whole nation safe, not just your tiny island of Manhattan, so if —"

"Adcock, it was me who had you brought up here, an *Irishman*. Now sit down and —"

"You made a request on paper for help from the Secret Service and you think making a simple request gives you the authority to tell the Secret Service anything at all? I'm the one who will be saying who's involved in this investigation. Not you."

Tunney gritted his teeth and stared at Adcock.

"You want to know who recruited this man? Colonel Roosevelt himself. Heard of him, Adcock? The former President of the United States?"

Adcock, for the moment, was the one who was silent.

"And I didn't make any paper request of anyone. The colonel and I called the White House and spoke to the Secretary of the Treasury, your boss, and told him the situation. His words to me were, 'Tom, we'll send a man up there to help you out.' To help me out. Understand that, Adcock? To help *me* out."

Adcock sat down but did not act chastised. "I don't know if you're aware, but I was head of the security detail that guarded President Wilson in Cleveland and Milwaukee last year. I was also in charge of the counterfeiting detection operations in the entire eastern United States region. I'm no simple agent. I presumed I was up here to take charge of this matter."

"Well, you presumed wrong. And you don't even know what this matter is, for God's sake."

"It remains to be seen who's in charge, but ..." When Tunney angrily began to answer, Adcock put up a hand. "... but I'll sit here and listen for today."

Tunney shook his head at the waste of time all this had been and regathered himself. "All right, first, I want John to tell you what he ... And listen, both of you. Nothing said in this room goes outside this room. Adcock, you have to report to your superiors and I understand that, but even in those reports, don't ever identify this man. There's German sympathizers all over both our departments, and I need this man protected because of how critical he is to this. Understand?"

Reluctantly, Adcock nodded.

Tunney turned to Nolan. "All right. Tell Adcock everything you've been doing. Bring him up to date. Then we'll start to formulate a plan."

Nolan told the entire story – the apartment in Hell's Kitchen, the arrest at the rally, the initial meeting with the lower ring of saboteurs, the New Jersey rail bombing, the trip to Bridgeport, the recruitment into the higher ring.

"In that meeting," Nolan said, "they talked mainly about Germany paying for labor strikes at U.S. war plants. The specific thing they said about the bombings is that it will be well before the Fourth of July."

Tunney turned to a calendar on the wall. "Sounds like April or May."

"And they said that a German explosives specialist has landed in Canada and will be in New York City in a week. The targets weren't —"

"What day was it said that he'll be in the city in a week?" Adcock asked.

"The meeting was four days ago, Monday, March sixth," Nolan said.

"So by this Monday he'll be here."

"Yes, but the targets weren't mentioned in the meeting and neither was the timing of the bombs. But one of them did say there'll be at least forty bombs, apparently all set to go off at once. One other thing that was mentioned was —"

"Forty individual bombs?" Tunney was incredulous.

"Yes."

"My God," Adcock said.

"But another thing was mentioned," Nolan continued. "There's a mill owner somewhere in Connecticut making

frequent purchases of both sulfuric and nitric acid which
they'll use to make TNT. Maybe someone could try to
find out who. Also, there's a watchmaker in the East making the timers and shipping them to New York City.
Watchmakers repair watches. They usually don't ship
them. Maybe it's possible for someone to look for a
watchmaker somewhere who is doing a lot of shipping to
the city lately."

When he finished, there was a thoughtful silence.
Then Adcock rose out of his chair and started pacing the
floor, shaking his head in disbelief.

"Forty bombs all going off at once," he said. "How do
we stop that? My God."

Tunney patted Nolan on the shoulder. "Good work,
John. You're just as good as I heard you were."

Packard Twin Six touring car

22

Crossing the Border

THEY LEFT MONCTON for the four-hour drive on a mix of paved and unpaved roads that would take them to Houlton, Maine, just over the border. Stopping on a country road at dusk near Fredericton, still in Canada, Haas drew a packed picnic basket from the rear seat. Wine, canned asparagus, and roast beef. They ate leaning on the motor's front fender.

"We'll be staying a few nights in Houlton with a friend, then we'll drive on to Arlington, Massachusetts. A wealthy German owns quite an estate in Arlington. One of the men from New York, the key men, will be driving up to meet us there. You'll have a chance to talk out the mission with him."

"These Germans we're staying with," Schwegel said. "Won't the government be watching them?"

"You can't watch all the Germans in America. There's millions of them. Because America's not at war, the government can't even register them. We're safe."

Well after dark, traveling on a deeply rutted road, Schwegel was nearly falling asleep in the passenger seat despite the rough going. Haas tapped him on the knee.

"We're close."

Haas extinguished the motor's headlamps, relying on light from a three-quarter moon to guide them. In another hundred yards, he pointed ahead to a cement obelisk on the roadside.

"There. That's the United States border."

A moment after they passed it, though, two large headlamps came on in front of them. They were those of a truck that blocked the entire road.

Haas stopped the Packard, and a man stepped down from the truck wielding a shotgun. He approached, the weapon leveled at them, and stood by the passenger window and Schwegel.

"Good evening, gents. Pretty late to be out running without lights on a road like this. Seems suspicious, don't you think?"

"Who are you?" Haas asked.

"The United States customs men employ me to guard this road, but there's never any traffic until the sun goes down, I've found, so that's why I come out here this time of night. Kind of strange, don't you think? A motor traveling without lights in the dark?"

"What do you want?"

Schwegel had slipped his left hand into his valise beneath his knees and was feeling for the Webley and the silencer. By feel alone and with one hand, he slowly screwed the silencer onto the barrel.

"Let me pose a question to you," the man with the

shotgun said. "Why are you running with no lights unless you want to get something into the United States illegally? Let me answer for you. You're trying to avoid customs duties. Am I right? But maybe we can negotiate a way out of your problem, if you tell me what it is you're smuggling."

"We're not smuggling anything," Haas said.

"You don't got a truck, so obviously it's something small. I'm guessing jewelry or gold or artwork. Am I right?"

Haas was silent.

Grinning at them, the man with the shotgun continued. "You might be paying customs up to sixty percent for things like that, but let's say, as just an idea, let's say you gave me thirty percent. Maybe we could work out a way to let you pass."

"We don't want to argue with you," Schwegel said, making the last turns of the silencer on the pistol barrel. "Here, I've got what we're carrying in my shaving kit. But when you split it up, remember. Only thirty percent. That's the agreement."

"I'll be fair, governor," he said smiling.

Schwegel leaned down as if to retrieve it from the valise. In fact, he did, taking his kit from it with his right hand and getting a good grip on the Webley with his left. He lifted the kit to the window then, as if the weight of the valuables caused him a moment of clumsiness, he dropped it so that it landed in the dirt at the man's feet.

"Oh, sorry," Schwegel said.

The man bent to pick it up up and, with a swift motion, Schwegel raised the Webley and fired right into the center of the top of the man's head, into a bald spot, creating an explosive spray of flesh, bone, and blood away from the motor. The man slumped to the ground instantly, coming to rest awkwardly against the motor. Haas got out and Schwegel, unable to force open his door because of the body, climbed across to get out the driver side.

Both of them stood over the dead man.

"Let's throw him into the weeds," Haas said.

They lifted him, one on the feet, the other gripping the hands, and carried him to the roadside, trying to avoid the stream of blood still coming from the center of his head. Then they begin to swing him for the toss.

"One, two … three."

The man twisted once in mid-air before landing on his back in tall, winter-wilted grass.

"I'll move the truck," Haas said.

Schwegel remained on the roadside. He gazed at the dead man whose face was illuminated by the moonlight, his eyes open, his mouth agape. There was no expression of pain or surprise. It was if the face had frozen a second before the bullet stunned and killed him, when only gold and jewels were on his mind.

Schwegel had the reaction then that he had come to know well. The personal assessment. How did this experience make him feel? It was the first time he had ever personally killed a man.

He realized, as he stood staring at the corpse, that he felt no sympathy or remorse, no sense of the magnitude of taking a human life. Instead, he felt exhilaration and the curious fascination one would have discovering a dead animal on a hike in the woods, a red deer or mountain hare perhaps, the body lying in the weeds, the rotting process underway, insects soon to invade its mouth and eat away at its eyes.

Was that all there was to killing? He had to shake his head. War might turn out to be a great adventure after all, he told himself. He had encountered one American and killed one American. Quite a record already.

Conrad, the man in charge

23

The Leak

"TOO LATE," BAUMANN said, handing Nolan the passport and driver's license. "The ink's already dry."

"I know a Liam Sweeney, though."

"From where?"

"From Ireland."

"Is he still in Ireland?"

"Far as I know."

"Well, O'Connell, in the United States of America, you're now Liam Sweeney."

Nolan examined the work as Baumann's engraver looked on, waiting for some acknowledgement of his efforts. A New York State driver's license and the passport. They stood in the rear of a printer's shop on West 34th Street.

"Looks very good," Nolan said.

"Your story is you crossed from Ireland in 1913," Baumann said. "So that's why the passport doesn't have a photograph. It was before the new law. Understand?"

Nolan nodded.

"One more thing for you." Baumann handed Nolan five one hundred dollar bills. Both Baumann and his engraver were beaming as he took them.

"Never seen one of these." Nolan said. In fact, he was not sure he ever had.

"Don't look too closely. They're counterfeit," Baumann said.

The engraver acted as if insulted. "No, you go ahead and look as close as you want. You won't find none better. There's threads in the paper, just like the real thing, and they run lengthwise, just like the real thing. You never see any of that in fakes."

"It's so you don't have to work and can pay your bills," Baumann said. "Take them over to Newark to the First Bank and ask for Boyle. He'll exchange them for you. You'll get back sixty real dollars for each. And I'd grow your beard longer so anyone knows you as O'Connell will have a harder time recognizing you. In fact, you might even shave it off."

"No, I want to keep it."

"Suit yourself. But move to a new flat on a different street. Don't start calling yourself Sweeney until you do, though. And better clothes. Spend some money and find a good tailor. I want you to be able to put Sweeney and O'Connell side by side and you would see completely different people. Understand?"

⊰※⊱

Five men were seated and talking as Baumann and Nolan arrived. The guard exited the storage locker and closed the massive oak door behind him. The room, in the steadily warming weather, had an even stronger stale smell than before.

"And how did they find out?" One of the men asked, part of a conversation already going on.

"We're not sure," said the man Nolan knew only as Conrad, the man in charge.

"Find out what?" Baumann asked.

"They found out the German has reached the United States. They know something big is being planned," Conrad said.

"Who found out?" Baumann asked.

"The New York police."

A silence followed and gradually Nolan understood what had happened. These men knew what he had told Tunney and Adcock. This sent a chill through him and his heart began to pound. However, no one was staring at him, so apparently they did not know he was the source of the police information.

"And how did you learn the police found out these things?" Baumann asked.

"We have a man at Rutherford who hears things," Conrad said.

"What's Rutherford?" Nolan whispered to the man next to him, who shushed him with a finger to his lips.

"But they don't know why he's coming and they don't seem to know about us. They just seem to know he's someone important," Conrad said. "My belief is the information came from Europe. Allied spies learned it and warned the Americans."

"Vat does dis change? Nutting," another man said, his German accented words barely understandable. "So dey know a man is coming from Germany? Vat help is dat to dem? Ve're no worse off."

"I bet I know how they found out," another man said with a scoffing attitude. "This damn German who's coming. I'll bet he's the one who couldn't keep his mouth shut."

There were nods of agreement from the others.

"When I heard they were bringing in an amateur to run the entire operation, someone to do the job Conrad should be doing, I knew this was wrong," said another.

"I heard he was only a chemist at an English university. He's never spent a day in the field. How old is he?"

"I'll bet he bragged to someone on the ship as he crossed that he thought was a friend to Germany – but wasn't." This man shook his head in disbelief and dismay, as did others.

Nolan felt the suspicions were landing elsewhere and not on him and he began to think more clearly. Either Tunney or Adcock was the leak. How could it be Tunney? He had hired Nolan, recruited him. He genuinely seemed to want to prevent these bombings. Adcock, though, seemed arrogant, enough so that it was believable he would slip and tell someone things he should not have.

And what was Rutherford? A company of some kind?

The meeting was mainly a report from one man about the effort to incite labor strikes on several docks in lower Manhattan where ships carrying munitions to Europe were berthed.

Afterward, as the meeting broke up, Conrad stopped Baumann outside the storage room to talk to him alone. Nolan waited further down the hall, his expectation growing.

"New orders," Baumann told Nolan as he joined him. "And they're coming from Becker."

"Who's Becker?"

"You just met him. Conrad. Conrad Becker. But the orders are that I'll come to these meetings alone from now on. You come if I can't. They're reducing the size of this group to only four, all of whom head a secondary group. They want the fewest people possible knowing the next step of the mission. It makes sense, what with this police thing that happened."

As they walked away, though, Nolan's mind worked frantically. Were these men such clever spies that they hid their suspicion of him through the entire meeting? Was his exclusion from the group the consequence of that suspicion? And was he to be followed and watched from this moment on? Or, worse still, assassinated?

The front desk at police headquarters

24

The News

"SAME DISGUISE AS last time," the desk sergeant said. "Go on up."

As Nolan climbed the stairs, he braced himself. His mind had not wandered from the idea that Adcock was the leak. However, his little time as a detective had taught him to not turn his back on any possibility. He had to suspect both men.

Tunney and a smiling Adcock were already seated in the conference room.

"Sit down, John. Adcock has some news. He —"

Adcock drew himself up in his chair. "*Some* news? It's not just *some* news."

Tunney rolled his eyes and turned again to Nolan. "We know the name of the German who's coming. Adcock was just about to tell me how it was discovered. Go ahead."

Adcock rose as if he had been invited to the podium of a stage. "We intercepted a coded telegram that was on its way to the German Embassy in Toronto. It was to be carried to the Consulate in New York in a diplomatic pouch, which it still will be. But our cryptologists broke the code in less than one day before having the telegram delivered to the Toronto embassy."

He handed both Tunney and Nolan typed copies of the decoded message.

> **Be advised that Robert McFee – his alias – is scheduled to arrive in New York City the week of March 12 to lead the coordinated bombings. Please extend him every courtesy and provide him as generous financial support as he might need. Bauer**

"This changes everything, of course," Adcock said.

"Changes what, other than we know who we're looking for?" Tunney said.

"The Secret Service is taking over this investigation. His targets may extend outside New York City. If it's as many bombs as your man here thinks —"

"You're not taking over anything," Tunney said.

"— they may have intentions to destroy national landmarks – the Washington Monument, the Statue of Liberty, even the White House. So this is a national situation. I want to —"

"Sit down, Adcock." Tunney glared at him.

Adcock did not move. Tunney sighed heavily, thought a moment, then rose and walked out of the conference room, muttering "wait here," as he did.

The silence he left behind quickly became awkward. Finally, Adcock turned to Nolan. "Give me your report.

Tell me what you've learned."

"I'd rather wait until the captain gets back," Nolan said.

Adcock exploded. "Damn it, man. If I tell you to give me your report, you give it. What are you anyway? Some foot patrolman telling me what you're going to do and not do?"

Nolan smiled and kept quiet. He was not even sure why he smiled, but Adcock saw it, was apparently puzzled enough by it that he seemed to think Nolan held cards he did not know about, so he just grunted and said nothing.

In a few minutes, Tunney returned. "I just got off the telephone with Secretary McAdoo." He turned to Nolan. "That's Adcock's boss." Then he turned back to Adcock. "You're to call him this afternoon for a little talk, Adcock. In the meantime, sit down and be quiet. What he told me is his department did not intercept this telegram. He said it was the Toronto police that intercepted it and the Canadians who decoded it. You were informed of it so that you could tell me about it and that's all."

"That's not the way I understood it. But regardless of how it happened, I still see this as a national situation now and if —"

"Adcock, sit down."

"I just think —"

"Sit down! Now!" Tunney shouted between clenched teeth.

Adcock sat, and for a few moments, as Tunney organized the papers in front of him and composed himself, there was silence.

Nolan was now convinced that Adcock was the source of the leak. There was something entirely earnest about Tunney that said he was not. However, it was his best guess that Adcock was unintentionally the source, that he was not deliberately passing along information to the Germans, that he was confiding in the wrong person, perhaps someone in the New York Secret Service office, a secret agent of Germany, who he unjustifiably trusted. He seemed thoughtless enough to do that.

Nolan feared this agent would try to wrestle more information from Adcock that would implicate Nolan, such as his description – the thick beard, about five feet nine, about thirty. If this were known, it would be the end of him.

"All right," Tunney said. "Enough time wasted. Let's make a plan. John, I don't know if this even concerns you. You have anything new?"

"Not at the moment."

"Then just go back to what you were doing and Adcock and I will deploy our men. We'll let you know how this will proceed at the meeting next week. But be aware that this man, this German, is on his way."

"One thing I would ask," Nolan said. "Under no circumstances should you tell anyone anything about me, what I look like, anything of a specific nature."

"You're telling *me* this?" Tunney said as if insulted.

"No, sir," Nolan said. "Not you … *him.*"

They both turned to Adcock who glared at Nolan. "And what's that supposed to mean?"

"Just a warning. Don't mention me to anyone. You can't trust people is what I'm saying."

Adcock shook his head dismissively, muttering something under his breath, as Nolan collected his coat to leave.

Huber welcomes them to breakfast

25

The New York Man

THE AGENT FROM New York, Schwegel was told, had already arrived and was downstairs in the kitchen, having breakfast. They were staying at an estate in Arlington, Massachusetts, owned by a German-born financier.

Schwegel washed and shaved. His face in the mirror was haggard, his eyes bloodshot. He had not been sleeping well. In Maine, the mattress was set on planks of wood and was too hard. Here in Massachusetts, the bedroom windows did not fully close and the bed had only one blanket. The March temperatures were cold enough that he never reached any depth of sleep.

Dressed, he went downstairs to the kitchen. Huber, the man who owned the estate, had donned a chef's apron and cap and was cooking eggs and bacon.

When Schwegel walked in, an older man briefly looked up from his plate then went back to eating. The New York man apparently. With his gray hair, he looked like someone's grandfather. Espionage could be quite physical. What good would this man be if there were trouble?

"Good morning. I'm Robert McFee."

The man stood and offered his hand. "Usually, I would say no names. Never any names. But I have to know yours and you have to know mine. It's Conrad Becker. I lead the New York groups."

"You already know my name," Huber said jovially. "What will you have – although since I've only got eggs and bacon, those are the only choices."

"Eggs and bacon then," Schwegel said. "Thank you."

He sat and was handed a plate of food and coffee. They were all silent as they ate. Huber turned once to see why they were not talking, but he just shrugged it off.

Finally Becker said, "McFee isn't your real name, is it?"

"No."

"Good. As I said, from now on, don't ever mention even your alias if you can help it. I'm here to educate you about how we do this sort of thing in America. And anonymity is critical."

Schwegel laughed derisively. "Anonymity is critical. I wouldn't have guessed that."

Becker only paused a moment at the sarcasm. "There're things you need to learn, McFee. It's why I'm here before you go much further. You just have to listen to me."

There was something deeply condescending in the man's tone, Schwegel thought. However, he decided to disregard it. The mission was the important thing, not petty personal conflicts.

"Another thing," the man said. "You —"

"Excuse me," Schwegel said. "If you don't mind, I'd just like to eat at the moment."

It had a sharp edge, and from Becker's reaction, the edge had caught him. Schwegel had not intended to say it; it had just jumped out of him. But so be it, he thought. How people treated him was important after all, he realized. He could not disregard it.

Becker glared at him a moment, then went back to his food, the kitchen again falling into silence.

Haas soon came down and was handed a plate of food. He and Huber immediately began talking about hunting. Haas had seen a large skunk foraging for roots on the lawn out his bedroom window just after dawn and the discussion got into whether you could shoot a skunk and keep it from spraying.

"Has to be a head shot," Huber said. "Never near the rear. The scent glands are right by its rectum. I learned this from experience."

"I hope we aren't spoiling these men's breakfasts," Haas said.

Becker smiled pleasantly as did Schwegel, but Haas seemed to detect the tension.

Finished with his breakfast, Becker stood. "Why don't we move our meeting into Herr Huber's library. There's some things I'd like to speak about."

"I'd like to have another helping of eggs," Schwegel said. "And Haas here, he hasn't finished."

Schwegel did not look up but noticed out the corner of his eye that Becker had not moved. He imagined he was being stared at, so he looked up challengingly.

"What I'm saying is I'll come in when I'm done. Then there's some things we should get clear regarding how this mission will be run." This also had a deliberate edge.

Becker, shaking his head, left. Schwegel could feel Haas' questioning gaze on him.

"What was that about?"

"Nothing important," Schwegel said.

When they finally arrived in the small library, Becker was seated in the only chair, a wingback, so Haas and Schwegel had to sit on a low couch, putting them a good foot below Becker. This was not lost on Schwegel.

Becker leaned forward as if about to lecture them. "I'd like to begin by acquainting you with some —"

Schwegel stood. "Sir, I don't know if you realize that the Abteilung IIIb sent me here to lead this mission, so I would appreciate it if you let me ask the questions, not you."

With a flash of anger, Becker stood. "What do you even know about America? Or New York City? You were a simple chemistry professor a few months ago. Is that not right?"

"You mean do I know anything about the very thing I've been trained for? Is that the foolish question you're asking?"

"I'm asking what you know about America."

Now Haas stood. "Gentlemen, please."

Becker waved him off. "I've been leading the New York situation for more than two years and I know things that an ... an outsider like you, someone barely out of school, doesn't even begin to know. That Germany would assign a ... a naive young man to step in —"

Furious, Schwegel began to interrupt, but Haas held his arm and interrupted himself. "Herr Becker, are you asking whether this man is a capable spy? If you are, I know the answer to that."

Becker threw up his hands. "He was only a professor before the war. How can —"

"We were all something before this war made us something else," Haas said. "But if you're asking whether he is a capable agent, let me tell you something, sir."

He told of the interception of the telegram to the War Office man during the crossing and the capture of the molds and the design for the new machine gun this led to in Halifax. Then he told of the midnight crossing of the border into Maine.

"As coolly and calmly as anyone I've ever seen, he killed this man and kept us on our schedule to get here. What exactly have you, the great expert in espionage, accomplished in the last week for Germany? Anything?"

His mouth trembling with anger, Becker remained silent.

"But gentlemen, please," Haas implored them. "Remember why we're here. *Germany*. Now let's begin again. And please, keep in mind the mission and only this mission."

Schwegel nodded agreement, but his mind was elsewhere. Becker had to be gotten rid of, he told himself, or at least pushed aside. Once in the city, he would take care of the matter himself.

Becker composed himself, then he drew a sheet from a hidden pocket inside his suit jacket. "We've worked very hard for this mission already in New York. We have targets, a good list, all carefully studied. For freighters, we can't know every one that will be in port when the time comes, but we already know several."

He held out the list to Haas, but Schwegel took it instead.

Dunholme - freighter, British, laden with case oil, Pier 51, Hoboken
Cygnet - Norwegian freighter, will be carrying 3,000 tons of munitions, berthed in South Brooklyn
Tyringdale - Pier 4 , Erie Basin, sugar, grains and shells. 3,700 gross tonnage

Also listed, along with a half dozen other freighters, were the residences of J. P. Morgan on Madison Avenue and John D. Rockefeller Jr. on West 54th Street, as well as New York City Hall on Broadway, Grand Central Terminal, the Woolworth building, the Metropolitan Opera House, Macy's, New York City police headquarters and the British and French embassies.

"We expect to have two dozen more shipping targets within a week of the bombings. Right now, we're building the chemist's laboratory you requested, a secret room in a building we control. I would advise that you stay here in Arlington until we finish."

However, Schwegel's attention was still on the list. "Do you have a pen?"

Becker hesitated a moment, then drew a Waterman pen from his inside pocket and handed it to him. Schwegel took the list and walked to the window, his back to the men. He made several annotations, scratching at the paper in quick, decisive strokes.

"We assembled that list very carefully," Becker said.

"I'm sure you did."

Now Schwegel returned with it and handed it back to Becker. He had eliminated many targets – Grand Central

Station, the Metropolitan Opera House, the Woolworth Building, Macy's. And Becker reacted instantly, his face turning red. "This is insulting. You think you —"

"Do you even want to know the reason why they were dropped before you go into a rage?"

Becker was putting on his overcoat to leave. "Not particularly."

"Well, there's a reason, a very good reason, and this is the reason."

Schwegel paused and Becker stopped what he was doing.

"Innocent women and children," Schwegel said.

A considerable silence followed.

"And what does that mean?" Becker asked, his anger still evident.

"If these bombings kill innocent women and children on Easter morning, and the people of New York look out the windows of their apartments or their automobiles and see bleeding women with their children, their dead babies, stumbling from a Grand Central Terminal or a Macy's or anywhere else, they'll be incensed. *Instantly*, they'll demand war. The very thing we're trying to avoid, we'll cause to happen."

Becker blew his nose into his handkerchief, absorbing what had been said. "I believe," he finally said, "there is just as much chance they will be so fearful that this could happen to them that they'll demand America stay out of war."

"Just as much chance? You want to leave this to chance? Absolutely not," Schwegel said. "We'll leave nothing to chance. Those targets will be dropped."

"Yet, you leave the personal residences of Rockefeller

and Morgan on the list. You leave the police headquarters, you leave City Hall," Becker said.

"Yes, I do. The average person thinks all these rich men should be shot anyway and they look at politicians as corrupt and at the police as their enemy. They might actually cheer if Rockefeller is blown up."

Haas laughed. "Great stuff, McFee. I agree with you completely."

However, Becker shook his head. "We carefully thought out this list and my people in New York —"

"Sir, they're *my* people now," Schwegel said. "Not yours."

Becker, his overcoat half on, sat in his chair again, the air taken out of him by Schwegel's clear reasoning and Haas' concurrence.

"I just want to go on record protesting this," Becker said.

However, the meeting was already moving on. Schwegel produced his bomb design, and spreading it out on the floor, he began to explain the workings of the device. One hundred pounds of trinitrotoluene or TNT. Steel or iron bomb casing. Rubber gaskets for waterproofing. The alloy magnets. A small charge of dynamite as the detonator. The mechanical timer.

As he was explaining the details of the bomb's manufacture, a telephone bell sounded in another room. In a moment, Huber was standing in the library door.

"Herr Becker. It's New York for you."

He left to take the call and Haas asked for a break to use the toilet. A moment after Haas returned, so did Becker.

"We have a change in the situation." Becker

announced, a subtle smile on his face. "The police have discovered your name, McFee. They know who you are and what you look like and why you're on your way to New York."

"That's not possible," Schwegel said.

"I have a man who finds out what the police know and they know all these things."

"Damn." Schwegel kicked the design sheet across the floor.

"So this is what must happen now," Becker said, vindication in his voice. "I instructed our people in New York to prepare a forged passport for you. You'll stay here in Arlington and when it's done, we can get you back to Canada where you can return to Scotland. This will take about a week. We can arrange passage for you. In the meantime, we will —"

"No," Schwegel said.

Becker laughed. "You're finished, McFee. You let your identity get out. I don't know how you did it, but you did."

"I didn't do any such thing. This could have been learned a dozen other ways. But no, I'm not going back to Scotland. I'm here and I'm staying here and this mission will continue."

"Aren't you the man who wants to leave nothing to chance? If the police know what you look like, how much chance does that add to this mission failing? Tell me that."

Schwegel thought a moment. "I'll grow a beard. I'll wear glasses. Your forgers can make me new papers."

"I won't jeopardize this mission because some young fool wants his personal adventure."

Schwegel jumped up. "I won't jeopardize this mission because some old fool is resentful that —"

"Stop!" Haas shouted. "I've had enough! This is finished! Done! However ... I agree with McFee. This mission can still be a success and I still believe he's the agent to do it. So Herr Becker ... Let McFee do his job."

Becker, seething, rubbed his eyes, and sat again, shaking his head. "This is madness. So much at stake. So much."

Haas smoothed out the design paper on the floor for Schwegel then gestured that he continue.

Adcock's residence in New Jersey

26

The Phone Tap

"**C**APTAIN TUNNEY, THIS is John Nolan. I'm calling to check in."

"What do you have for me?"

"I'm mainly calling to find out when the next meeting is." Nolan was at the public phone in the Hotel Flanders near his new apartment in Hell's Kitchen. He had moved only a few blocks away, to West 49th Street, but the conditions were no better. A common bathroom and cold water spigot out in the hallway.

"Next Tuesday, but in the afternoon, say two o'clock. There's a trolleymen's strike in New Jersey and Adcock can't get here until the afternoon. He's staying with his brother in Rutherford."

"Rutherford? Is that a town?"

"In New Jersey, yes."

"I ... I'll be there at two."

As he rushed back to his apartment, he became so caught up in his thoughts that when a bluecoat stopped him on the street to ask his name and to feel for a revolver ("Why ain't you working this time of day, Mick. You got a night job I should know about?") he had to think twice about who he was. Nolan? O'Connell? Sweeney?

Managing to avoid arrest, he got home and found the slip of paper hidden in the ice box with the telephone number of the agent, Michaels, he had worked with on the rail bombing in New Jersey. Michaels worked for the Secret Service in the Manhattan office, the office Adcock was working from while in New York.

Then he returned to the Hotel Flanders to make another call. A voice answered on the second bell. "This is Michaels."

"I hope you remember me. This is John ..." Nolan hesitated. "I mean James O'Connell. The undercover man who worked with you in New Jersey. I'm going by the name Liam Sweeney at the moment, though."

"Sure. How are you, Sweeney?"

He told Michaels about the Germans saying they were getting information about police espionage investigations from a man in Rutherford and that Adcock was staying in Rutherford.

"I'm guessing the Germans have a telephone tap of some kind on Adcock's line," Nolan said. "Either that, or Adcock's brother is the source. I don't think it's Adcock himself. At least I hope not."

There was silence on the line for a long moment.

"It's almost noon," Michaels finally said. "There's an automobile ferry that crosses the Hudson from 42nd Street to Weehawken on the Jersey side. Can you meet me in two hours at the 42nd Street landing? I'll drive."

"I'll be there, but I have to be back by five. The

Germans are meeting tonight. What about Adcock?"

"He's in meetings here in New York all day, so that won't be a problem."

———※———

On the ferry, sitting in Michaels' runabout while they crossed the river in a warm drizzle, they talked out the possibilities. One was that either Adcock's brother or his sister-in-law was a German sympathizer and was passing along information. Another was that German agents in Washington, perhaps even in the bureau, had learned Adcock was staying in Rutherford while assigned to the Manhattan office. If so, maybe other agents rented the apartment next to Adcock's – or above or beneath it – to listen through the walls or to tap his telephone line.

Once across the river, they stopped first at the public library in Rutherford and went through the telephone directory. There was only one Adcock listed – 268 Union Avenue. They also looked at the library's copy of the voter registration rolls. Only one Adcock was on that list as well, with the same address.

They parked across the street on Union Avenue. A neat, brown three-decker with one apartment to a floor. Lights were on only in the first floor. Despite several recent snowstorms, the weather had warmed enough in recent days that much of the snow had melted and the brown lawn had emerged in spots. The drizzle was quickly eliminating the snow that was left.

Michaels cranked down his window and squinted. "There's an 'apartment for rent' sign in the first-floor window. Let's see what that's about."

With the wind blowing and pelting them with rain, they both went to the front door. Michaels knocked and an elderly man, lean and muscular the way lifelong laborers often are, opened it.

"You the landlord?" Michaels asked. "I saw your sign. Any chance we can take a look at the apartment?"

With a suspicious gaze, the man studied them. "I guess. Let me get my keys."

"Don't say anything," Michaels whispered to Nolan when the man disappeared inside. "He hears you're Irish, he might not show it to us. Let me do the talking."

As they climbed the stairs, the landlord told them the tenant had died two months earlier.

"So this has been empty for two months?" Michaels asked.

"It was winter so it took a month to finally smell he was dead, so it's been empty a month." The landlord unlocked the door and motioned them in. "Which one of you is looking to rent?"

"I am," Michaels said. "What'd he die of?"

"Carrot juice."

"What?"

"He drank only carrot juice to keep his health and he drank so much of it that it ruined his liver."

"Whiskey could have done the same thing but been a lot more fun," Michaels said. "Can you tell me something about the other tenants?"

"A fellow and his wife on the second floor. The Adcocks. Nice people. They both work. I'm alone on the first floor. I'm retired."

The apartment was barren of any furniture and smelled of a fresh scrubbing with bleach.

"Do the apartments have telephones?" Michaels asked.

"Each apartment has a line. Whether they hook up is their business. I have one and I think the Adcocks have one."

"Is there storage space in the basement? Can we see that? I'm being transferred here from Chicago and I've got more stuff than can fit up here."

The landlord sighed at the imposition, but after locking up, he led them down and around to the back of the house. The drizzle had stopped momentarily, but the warm March wind was still gusting. He opened the basement hatchway with a second key hidden under a rock.

"Watch your heads. I don't like going down there 'less I have to. I've got lung disease and the coal dust bothers me bad enough already. But there's a hurricane lamp and matches right inside the door, if you want to look around."

They found the telephone junction box behind the furnace. Michaels slowly swept the lamp across it then stopped when he saw a pair of brown wires leading out of the box. The other wires were sheathed in dark green fabric.

"The telephone company uses only green wires. Those brown wires aren't theirs," Michaels said. "Looks like a tap. It must be your Germans."

With his index finger, Michaels followed the brown wires over to the foundation, which was constructed of boulders cemented together. His finger stopped where a hole had been drilled in the flaking cement so the wires could get to the outside.

In the back yard again with the landlord, Michaels pulled out his Secret Service badge. The man had a stunned expression when he saw it and as he listened to

Michael's explanation of the wire tap.

They discovered where the wires left the basement foundation and dropped down to the dirt. From there, they were buried, but it was an easy matter to trace their shallow path across the lawn – directly toward the house next door. Fortunately, the three men were hidden from view of the other house by a thick line of overgrown yews between the houses.

"Let's go inside," Michaels said.

In the kitchen, Michaels studied the other house through the window. "Do you know who lives there?"

The landlord shook his head. "They got new tenants it seems like every few months."

"You're not under suspicion, sir, but I'm going to have to set up in here for a few days. I have to drop this man off at the ferry, then I'll come back."

"I guess so if you have to," said the clearly agitated landlord.

"However, it's critical that you don't tell your second-floor tenants that anything is going on. They can't know and they especially can't know I'm here. I think they're why the tap was put on."

Baumann pushed aside the silverware and opened the map on the table. They were in a back booth at the Walhalla Garden, a German restaurant on First Avenue. He turned the sheet to Nolan and pointed.

"Right here in Hoboken. It was a cotton warehouse, but now it's being used as temporary storage for munitions and most of the night it's unguarded. Lots of kegs of powder and cases of shells are coming to New Jersey by train, but they're running out of places to store it all until it can be shipped out. That's what we want to blow up sometime next week after a big shipment is scheduled to come in."

Nolan studied the map. "I know that neighborhood. There's houses and businesses all around it. The post office is right down the street."

"So?"

"So if we blow it up and all those kegs and shells explode, the whole neighborhood will go up."

Baumann smiled. "So?"

"Have you calculated how many people will die?"

Baumann smirked at Nolan's concern. "This is war, for God's sake. Besides, it's been approved by everyone above me. They want this done."

Nolan pretended to study the map. He did not want to appear unwilling to do the job. He had come too far to lose Baumann's confidence now. "Then all right," he said with conviction. "What do you want me to do?"

That pleased Baumann. "We just want you to ride along to give my group a report. We have three young men, very ambitious men, who will set the charges. It'll be after midnight when there are no guards around. The beauty of this is that there are so many kegs of powder in that warehouse that when they set off one, the others will blow instantly. It's like these fools are handing us a ready-made bomb. We'll make it look like the place exploded on its own. So if people die, it'll be blamed on them for storing explosives in a crowded neighborhood, not us."

Michaels reads from the transcript

27

The Leak Revealed

WEARING HIS WIG and glasses, Nolan arrived early at police headquarters Tuesday afternoon and waited in the lobby, which was crowded with patrolmen and their rough-looking suspects. The desk sergeant seemed to recognize him – or at least his disguise – and barely looked up from his newspaper.

When Nolan saw Adcock enter, he turned away, hiding his face. Adcock, holding up his federal badge for the desk sergeant to see, went right upstairs.

Nolan looked at the clock above the booking desk, anxiously waited a few minutes longer – even going out to the street and searching up and down the sidewalk – before he went upstairs as well.

Tunney was not there yet. Adcock, pacing the conference room, only briefly turned, but did not acknowledge him.

Now Tunney came in. "All right. Let's get down to work."

"Sir," Nolan said. "There might be one more person coming. Can we wait a couple of minutes?"

"Who?" Tunney asked.

At that moment, Michaels stuck his head in the door, looked at Nolan, then saw Adcock.

"What the hell are you doing here?" Adcock demanded.

"He's with me," Nolan said.

"This man works for me! Not for you, damn it! Who the hell do you think you are using my men without asking me! Tunney, for God's sake, why —"

"I don't know this man or anything about him," Tunney said.

"Sir," Nolan said. "There's an explanation."

Michaels, a sheepish expression on his face, had not budged from the doorway.

"Then let's hear it," Tunney said. He turned to Michaels. "Might as well come in."

Michaels, carrying a thick folder, took a seat next to Nolan. Adcock, staring furiously at Michaels, refused to sit.

"I didn't tell you this," Nolan said. "But in one of the meetings with the Germans, a man got mentioned, a man the Germans said could find out everything the police knew."

"A man in my department?" Tunney said.

"No sir. They said it was a man … in Rutherford."

With that, everyone turned to Adcock who glared back at them as if insulted. "You think I —"

"No, not you," Nolan said. "But the Germans had a tap on the telephone line into your brother's apartment. So I asked Michaels to tap the tappers."

Adcock's face grew ashen and he took a seat.

Michaels drew a bound transcript from the folder. "We set up a dictograph on the tap line and had a stenographer take down what she heard over several days. The important calls were those that Agent Adcock made. On page six … well, I guess I'll just read it." He cleared his throat. "This is Agent Adcock speaking to Agent Kitwell, the man under him at the Washington bureau. This call was on March twenty-fourth, four days ago. Quote. And this starts with Adcock … Quote. If you have to tell the secretary something, tell him I've been personally tracking any shipments of nitric and sulfuric acid, which is for TNT, into New York City … Now this is Kitwell speaking. Yes sir. Now Adcock again. And did you go by my apartment and water my geraniums? Kitwell. Yes, sir. Now Adcock —"

Suddenly, Adcock shot out of his chair, having had enough. "You tapped my telephone line and you didn't tell me about it? I swear, you're as good as fired Michaels, and I'll —"

Tunney shot out of his chair also. "For God's sake, Adcock. You could have been the German agent, so how the hell can they tell you they're investigating you? Quit threatening this man or I'll get *you* fired, you damned fool. I know for a fact you're supposed to make all your official calls to Washington on the direct line from the Secret Service's office in Manhattan. That's why they put that line in there. It can't be tapped."

"If I go down to that office when I'm uptown, I'll never make it home to New Jersey in time for dinner."

For a moment, Tunney could not speak he was so astonished, so outraged. "So you're telling me you put the security of this country at risk by making your official calls from this damned apartment house in Rutherford, and you never took the simple precaution of checking to make sure the line wasn't tapped? You did this because you wanted to be home in time for your supper? Is that what you're saying?"

Adcock seemed to finally realize what he had done. He dropped back into his chair, mumbling under his breath and lowering his head.

"Let's see that damned transcript," Tunney said.

Michaels slid it across the table. Tunney leafed through the pages, stopping momentarily to read.

"You keep mentioning my name, Adcock. For God's sake. I told you never to use my name outside this room ... God, Adcock. You use your people to buy birthday gifts for your nephews? And this ... Kitwell, see if you can get me baseball tickets for the opener next month in New York against Washington."

"Please, don't call the secretary," Adcock whispered, his disgrace final.

"Sir, if I can say something," Nolan said. "Right now the Germans don't know we're onto this tap. We can use that. We can use agent Adcock to plant information with them we want them to have. And right now there's one thing in particular that would help us if they heard it."

"What's that?"

"Baumann, Henrik Baumann. A vicious bastard and the man I report to. But if he was eliminated, I'd probably move up a rung on the ladder."

The plan they arrived at was this. Adcock would call Washington that evening from Rutherford and read from a script that Nolan would write for him. He would say that a German, Henrik Baumann, was close to agreeing to become a police informer, that he may know something about the bombings and was being promised money and sanctuary in Canada if he agreed to work for the police.

"Then you'll say you're meeting with Baumann three days from now to get his answer and we might have some names and details by the end of the week."

Tunney looked at Adcock. "Can you do this?"

Adcock nodded, barely raising his head.

"One other thing," Nolan said. "The Germans want a warehouse in Hoboken bombed Saturday night."

Tunney turned to the wall calendar. "April first."

"Apparently it's filled with explosives waiting to be shipped out," Nolan said. "And they want me to go along to give a report to them. The problem is that if I want to stay high in their regard, I have to go."

Tunney weighed this. "I can't let you blow up a warehouse."

"I don't intend to," Nolan said. "But I have a plan."

"Then let's hear it."

Saboteurs in the alley

<h1 style="text-align:center">28</h1>

<h1 style="text-align:center">The Hoboken Plot</h1>

"WHAT DO YOU have to do that late at night?" Sheenagh asked.

"I have to watch a warehouse … to see if any suspicious things are going on. But I'll be home Sunday night." Nolan was at the public phone at a hotel on Third Avenue.

"What if you see some suspicious thing? What do you do then?"

"I just write it down in my diary and report it to Captain Tunney."

"So you don't have to rush in and stop this suspicious thing. You don't have to use a gun or anything."

"No, Sheenagh. Nothing I do is that dangerous, but it has to be done."

In these telephone calls, he always understated the peril. Nevertheless, she was quiet in her disapproving way, but he knew to wait it out.

"Then I'll stay up late for you Sunday," she said. "I

wish this were over. I miss you."

"I want this over as much as you, believe me. I'll see you Sunday night. I've got to go. I love you."

—◆◈◆—

Nolan drove a machine Baumann stole for them in the Bronx, a Chevrolet touring model bearing a license plate lifted from another motor. The moonlit night was warm for the first of April. They took a late ferry over to New Jersey, had dinner at a seafood restaurant in Fort Lee, then drove down to Hoboken after midnight.

The three men with Nolan, all young Germans, knew him as Sweeney. It was their first bombing. Much of their talk during dinner and the drive was in German, even though they spoke reasonable English. From the excitement in their voices and their nervous laughter, Nolan could guess what they were saying. Dumb Americans. Won't they be surprised.

Dumb Germans, Nolan thought. Won't you be surprised.

One after another, snowstorms had swept up the East Coast during March. However, the warm temperature that day had filled the unlighted back roads with puddles, making the driving treacherous. Nolan feared they would not reach Hoboken by one o'clock in the morning – the time he told Tunney he would be there.

The warehouse was squeezed into a neighborhood of tenements and other industrial buildings by the Hudson River.

Nolan parked the Chevrolet in the service alley that ran alongside the warehouse and into the building's small parking lot where Tunney's men were waiting in their motors. It was lit by the full moon and one electric security light high on the building. And as was prearranged with Tunney, he flashed his headlamps twice before switching them off. His passengers were too busy getting out of the Chevrolet to notice.

One of the Germans had a valise filled with the dynamite and the fuses, and he and Nolan went to the building's alley door. The other two Germans waited by the machine.

Nervous about what he knew was about to follow, Nolan had told Tunney specifically what he would be wearing.

At the padlocked side door, the German put a small crowbar to work on the iron lock. Seconds later, two of Tunney's detectives were in the alley with their guns drawn.

"Raise your hands. All of you. What's going on here?"

However, Nolan saw one of the men by the Chevrolet reach into his jacket. He started to yell a warning, but the revolver was out too quickly and shots began flying. More of Tunney's men, nearly a half dozen, were immediately out of their machines and firing, and in twenty seconds, if that, it was over.

As the last shots were fired, Nolan felt a blow to his leg, like he had been kicked. He glanced down to see a spreading stain of red on his pants just below the knee, on the calf. He felt little at first, just a tingling numbness, then, as if his body suddenly realized what had happened, the searing pain started, like the worst burning imaginable.

All three Germans were down on the bricks as was one of Tunney's detectives, grasping his hand. Two of the Germans were not moving and a detective was kneeled down, feeling for a pulse of the third. Shot twice in the chest, the German was slowly writhing on the pavement.

"I'm afraid those two are dead," the detective on his knees said. "This one will be soon. You don't survive wounds like this. We need to get him to a hospital."

Now Tunney noticed Nolan's wound. "John, you've been shot," Tunney said. "Someone get the medical kit from my motor. Let's try to keep this one German alive also."

However, as one of Tunney's men went for the kit, the German stopped breathing and his face drained of color. "Never mind," Tunney said.

The pain throbbing, Nolan raised his bloody pants leg so Tunney could see the wound. Blood flowed from a shallow gulley of exposed, raw, pink flesh inches below the knee.

"Hopefully, it wasn't one of my men," Tunney said. "They knew not to fire at you. Either it was a German or a ricochet. Hurts like hell, I'll bet."

"Like hell or worse," Nolan said, gritting his teeth.

"It isn't deep. Looks like you only got grazed. You won't even need stitches," Tunney said. "But God, those things bleed, don't they."

The kit arrived, salve was applied, and a bandage was wrapped tightly around the thigh. Nolan was also given a dose of laudanum.

The wounded detective had been hit in the hand. A bullet caught the tip of his thumb, perhaps breaking the bone. He only required bandages until he could get to the hospital.

The shooting had awakened many in the neighborhood. Kerosene lamps and electric lights could be seen coming on in various windows. Two detectives were sent to keep away the curious.

Tunney helped Nolan to the nearest motor, the Chevrolet Nolan had driven.

"Captain, we have a problem," Nolan said as he sat in the passenger seat. "How am I going to explain this to the Germans? I'm the only one not dead."

Nolan's plan had been to allow himself to be arrested with his three confederates, then Tunney would arrange for him and one of the others to escape during the transfer either to jail or to court for arraignment. Nolan would then tell Baumann they were ambushed at the warehouse, that guards had been added for the overnight shift, something the other man with him would vouch for.

"I guess this is a problem," Tunney said. He gazed at Nolan distractedly, as if hatching a new plan. He turned to his detectives. "You two bring one of the Germans over here."

The men picked up the smallest dead body and, trying to keep the blood off themselves, they carried it over to the Chevrolet.

"Put it in the back seat," Tunney said. "John, you can't go back with us. You wouldn't have a plausible story about how you convinced the ferrymen to take two blood-soaked men over to Manhattan without calling the bluecoats. So this is what you've got to do. First, are you going to be well enough to drive?"

Nolan already felt the pain diminishing. He nodded.

"Wait until dawn then call this Baumann and tell him you were ambushed and shot, but you and one of the Germans escaped. You tell him you broke into a pharmacy for bandages, but the German with you badly needs a doctor."

Nolan glanced at the dead man. "Real badly, I would say."

"You tell Baumann to come over and pick you up. When he gets there, you tell him the other man will corroborate your story. When Baumann goes to question him, he'll be dead. It will make your story sound real, though. You figure out the rest of it. Have him get you to a doctor too, John."

⊷⊰⊱⊶

The story was on the front page of the *Evening Herald* the next day.

TWO SABOTEURS KILLED, TWO ESCAPE

Their target was a New Jersey munitions warehouse

A plot to blow up a waterfront warehouse in Hoboken was foiled early this morning by alert security guards who spotted four men trying to gain entry by a locked door in the side of the building.

In a rapid-fire gun battle, two of the plotters were shot and killed instantly while two others were shot but escaped in their own machine. The blood-splattered motor, which had been stolen yesterday in New York City, was found abandoned in Fort Lee hours later.

The names of the dead men, who carried

no identification papers, is not known. Both were believed to be in their early twenties and appeared Teutonic, according to a police statement. Several sticks of dynamite and cord fuses were found in a valise on the ground near their lifeless bodies.

There have been a string of warehouse bombings along the waterfront in recent months, believed to have been instigated by supporters of the German cause in the European war.

Inspecting the laboratory

29

The Hidden Laboratory

THE METALWORKS FACTORY, owned by a German named Fischer, was on West 38th Street. Schwegel, his thinning hair and scruffy beard dyed black, was being led to the basement by a half dozen men, including Becker, Fischer, and a large bodyguard.

Silently, they walked through a storage area holding piles of scrap metal and wood, then past a furnace and coal bin. Directly behind the furnace was a brick wall. However, the wall was less dirty, less coated with black coal dust, than any others in the basement, as if it had been constructed more recently.

The bodyguard pushed aside a thin metal sheet leaned against the wall to reveal a door painted and textured to look like bricks. A hidden room was on the other side.

"One thing," Schwegel said. "You'll have to blacken this newer wall to make it look like the others or else someone looking for the laboratory will spot what's going on immediately. I'm surprised you didn't think of that."

"Of course we thought if it," Becker said. "We plan to do it this week. We've thought of everything, my young friend."

The door was opened to reveal a sophisticated laboratory with electric lights, running water, shelves with labeled bottles of chemicals, a long wooden workbench with drawers, blowtorches, soldering irons, Bunsen burners, beakers, test tubes, rolls of copper wire, rolls of sheet metal, and two dozen timers fashioned from clocks atop a second workbench.

With no comment, Schwegel entered and began examining everything, taking a slow walk around the room. Becker trailed behind him, triumphant in his elaborate preparations.

Schwegel stopped at the shelves, reading the labels. They were all acids – hydrochloric, sulfuric, nitric, acetic, hydrofluoric, carbolic, and muriatic.

"We don't need some of these. Why are they even here? They just take up space," Schwegel said.

Becker grimaced at the criticism. "We didn't know what you needed, so we prepared for anything. Some of these acids are hard to get in quantity on short notice. The police check the shipments."

"Well, I'm telling you now we don't need them. Get rid of them. Sulfuric acid and nitric acid – we need *more* of them. We don't need the hydrofluoric, the carbolic."

Becker turned to the owner, shaking his head. The ingratitude of the man. However, Schwegel saw this and bristled.

"In the future," Schwegel said. "I only want to deal with one of you. Not you, Herr Becker." He pointed to one of Becker's other men. "You. What's your name?"

"I'm Voigt, but it's Herr Becker who you should be talking to. He recruited all of us and has been running da operation."

"No, you're the man I'll deal with, Voigt. Now, some other things I'll need. I want —"

"Sir," Voigt said with his heavy German accent. "Herr Becker is da only man who knows everyting and everyone. He knows vere we get materials. He knows da targets, da shipping schedules, da police who are friendly to us, everyting."

The others all nodded or mumbled some word of agreement. Becker eyed Schwegel as if to say, "You've been told the truth. What does a man like you do with that truth once you have it? Do you put the good of the Fatherland above everything else?"

Schwegel looked away momentarily, studying the timing clocks. Without looking back at the men, he said, "All right, Just Becker then … Now, other things. I don't plan to go out much, so I'll sleep down here. I want a cot, blankets, and a chamber pot for the nights. I assume there's a toilet and a sink upstairs somewhere for other times. I also want an ice chest for food down here. And I want some good German beers and wines and some knackwurst and bratwurst." He pointed at the windows. "And these windows, you need to blacken them so no one can look in here."

"The windows, of course, are something else we plan to do this week. As I told you, we've thought of everything," Becker said with pride, as if he had won something back, however small.

The explosives, two and a half pounds of TNT, would be held inside a steel canister, which would be fashioned upstairs in the machine shop by Fischer's workers. As Becker and his men went off to collect the food and other supplies that Schwegel demanded, he detailed to Fischer the container he would require.

"I need it shaped like a milk bottle, but flat on one side, where the magnets will be attached. We'll need forty of them." He held his blueprint open on a workbench while Fischer, nearly seventy Schwegel guessed, wrote down the exact measurements.

"You say the magnets are cobalt and steel?" Fischer asked.

"Yes, tungsten steel."

"We can make those too. Round disks it looks like here. Are you an engineer?"

"A chemist."

"I myself am an engineer. For someone who hasn't the training, this is reasonably good work."

Schwegel grimaced. How arrogant, how condescending.

"Let me guess how this will work," Fischer said. "This is your timer here. Correct? … When the time comes, it triggers this spring here, which shoots out this bolt into … looks like a rifle cartridge. That fires into this small charge of dynamite, and that explosion sets off the bigger charge of TNT. Correct?"

Schwegel nodded again. So he could read a blueprint. So what?

"Perhaps I can suggest something," Fischer said.

Schwegel had had enough. "Sir, this was designed and tested by the best German engineers, so I seriously doubt you could possibly add anything of value."

"Perhaps I can, though. You said you tested it on the Havel in August. Here, in April, the water temperature on the Hudson River is near freezing. It's water that's flowed down to the city from the Adirondack Mountains, so it's meltwater from snow on those peaks. And your bomb will be sitting underwater for a good twelve hours. Have you taken into account the effect of the cold temperature on your method of detonation? If you have lubricants in this design, they may be affected."

"Of course I've thought of that, for God's sake."

"I meant no insult, sir. It's just that a lot's at stake."

In silence, Fischer continued studying the blueprint. However, Schwegel's mind was racing. In fact, he had not considered the effect of the water temperature and he was sure the engineers in Berlin had not either. He would have to do some quick research and refiguring.

———❦———

Just before dusk, as the metal shop upstairs emptied of workers, Schwegel put on his thick glasses and an oversize overcoat and went for a walk. He strolled along the waterfront as longshoremen and others ended their shift for the day, walking home in small knots of men – Italians with Italians, Irishmen with Irishmen, he guessed as he listened to the languages and accents as they passed.

He studied the freighters in their berths, the closest being the *SS Durham* at the 39th Street pier. The overnight crew was scurrying about the deck, loading cargo with winches and ropes, perhaps crates of bullets and shells bound for the Allies, thinking themselves so safe, so beyond the reach of the war. America – reaping mighty profits from the conflict but refusing to get its hands dirty. America, he told himself, will finally get what it deserves.

Conrad Becker

30

A Visit by Becker

T HE KNOCKING ON the door of his apartment in Hell's Kitchen was so quiet that he barely heard it above the noise from the noontime street traffic. Finally, Nolan investigated, standing close to the door.

"Who's there?"

"I'm a friend of a friend who you know well."

Hearing the slight German accent, he unbolted the door. It was Becker and another man.

"Herr Becker. I was expecting Henrik," Nolan said. "Is something wrong?"

"Nothing's wrong, but Herr Baumann has been transferred out of New York."

"To where?"

"To ... well, we don't want to reveal it. But it's something important we need his talents for. I know he recruited you and you probably have warm feelings toward him, but you have to realize this is wartime and you have to adjust."

Nolan had to keep himself from smiling. "I understand completely."

"By the way, my friend here is an important associate of mine. Herr Voigt."

Voigt nodded at Nolan who nodded in return.

"But your situation has changed," Becker said. "You'll be our connection to my planing group from now on. You're becoming a valuable asset, Mr. O'Connell. You've handled your missions well and we appreciate it."

"Actually, I've been going by the name Sweeney, Liam Sweeney. I have new papers."

"O'Connell is how we knew you in our group, but … Sweeney then. By the way, how's your leg?"

"It's healing."

"Can we see it?"

No one had asked to see it to that point, so Nolan could finally show it off. He raised his pants leg to the knee. Just four days old, the scab was large, ugly, and crusted over.

"Impressive," Becker said, nodding his head in admiration. "You have your badge of honor, Mr. Sweeney. However, we have a new mission for you. We need you to take several motor trips to Norwalk, Connecticut. You have to pick up additional bottles of acids that we need for our Easter man."

"Your Easter man?"

"The man planning the Easter bombings."

"I see."

"You've heard us talk about a day of coordinated bombings? They're being planned for Easter morning."

Nolan nodded as if this was not important news to him, just news, but in the back of his mind, he was calculating the days until Easter – less than three weeks.

Becker continued. "A German who owns a factory in Norwalk has been getting small shipments of nitric and sulfuric acid for us. It's for TNT. We need you to drive up there and pick up some new bottles he's gotten, taking only two bottles at a time. It's an amount you can hide in your motor. And if you're stopped and they're found, that might not get you arrested. Another man will accompany you, name of Hauxthausen."

"Someone mentioned you're preparing a laboratory for building the bombs. Will we take the bottles there?"

"No. You'll drop them in a storage room we've rented on 67th Street. We have a man who will pick them up there to take to the lab. They want as few people as possible knowing where this lab is. We're looking into a rumor there's a traitor gotten into our group."

This froze Nolan. "Who?"

"We think it's one of the men in a lower group, but we're looking into it. We have a man in the police department who hears things, and he heard something. So don't repeat any of the information I give you to anyone. Understand?"

Nolan nodded.

"Here. This paper has the addresses in Norwalk and the storage room for the chemicals on 67th."

"Will the storage room be locked?"

"We'll have a man there from seven o'clock to midnight every evening this week with a key. And here's another paper. You'll meet Hauxthausen at this address, an empty lot in the Bronx, the day after tomorrow at four in the afternoon. He'll have a motor for you. It will take four or five evenings to get all the bottles. They'll be heavily packaged and labeled as engraving acids. They're not explosive by themselves. Do you understand all this?"

"Yes."

Becker smiled and grasped Nolan's arm paternally. "Herr Baumann was very sorry he didn't have time to see you before he left, but he said to wish you well and to thank you for your service to Germany."

"If you see him again, thank him for me. Will you do that?"

Carrying the cedar chest home

31

The Choice

NOLAN SLEPT LATE, waking to find that Sheenagh was already up. He could smell bacon cooking in the kitchen.

Sunlight, finding a narrow path into the alley between their building and the next, streamed into the window. It managed to push through the layered grime on the glass pane and through the sheer linen curtains Sheenagh had sewn herself, as if the light owned a mission to brighten his bedroom.

He savored the moment. The loveliness of this morning, this bed. Was the mattress any softer than the one in his apartment on 49th Street? Probably not. Yet, in his mind, it was infinitely so.

Then his thoughts went to Becker's rumor of the traitor and his pleasure was stopped cold.

He had been taking convoluted routes to reach both his Brooklyn home and Tunney's office in Manhattan to throw off anyone who might be following him – cutting through alleys, going in the front door of taverns and out the back, changing subways or streetcars multiple times.

Becker had acted as if Nolan were not suspected at all, but spies acted; that's what they did best. Would he have told Nolan about a traitor if Nolan were a suspect? Not likely.

Becker said the rumor came from their man in the police department, perhaps someone right in Tunney's department. He lay in bed trying to think of what more he could do to avoid detection, but there was not any precaution that he had not already taken.

What was it his father used to say? Worry only about what you can change, not what you can't. Whatever was going to happen was going to happen, he told himself. He had done the best he could.

As he pulled on his pants, he checked the gauze bandage on his leg. No sign of blood. The wound was now a week old. Coming home the night after the shooting, as he undressed in the moonlit bedroom, Sheenagh had seen it and asked what had happened. He had told her he scratched it on the sharp edge of his coal stove in the other apartment. In the dim light, she had not noticed it was an impossible explanation for a bandage that large.

Now he drifted toward the scent of bacon and the whistle of the tea kettle. He had come home the previous night to celebrate – a day late – his and Sheenagh's birthday, which both fell on the same day, April sixth. He turned twenty-nine. She turned twenty-five.

Sheenagh, at the stove, glanced back. "How did you sleep, birthday boy? And are you going to be able to stay around today? I need your help with something."

"And how are you, dear?" He kissed the back of her

neck as she stood at the stove. "And happy birthday to you too, birthday girl."

She wriggled free. "John, stop. I've got a hot skillet here. Are you going to be able to stay around all day?"

Through her housecoat, the baby was beginning to show. He thought it adorable. "Just 'til after lunch, 'til about three."

"What's going on after lunch?"

"I have to drive up to Connecticut this afternoon with another man."

"But until then, you can stay? I need you to go somewhere with me after breakfast."

"I'm at your beck and call." He kissed her neck again, and this time she let him, but with a free hand he reached into the skillet, braving the hot grease to grab a strip of bacon.

———————

Across the East River from Manhattan, Brooklyn had become its own bustling city. Forty years earlier, it could be reached from lower Manhattan only by ferries and was known for its churches, cemeteries, and rural charm. However, with the addition of so many bridges and subway lines across the river, the borough was sleepy no longer. New buildings seemed to be going up in every available space. And on a shopping day, such as this, crowds filled the sidewalks and the stores.

The small cedar chest Sheenagh wanted was in a curiosity shop on Myrtle Avenue, a half dozen blocks from their apartment. Once it was paid for, Nolan hoisted it on his shoulder and they began the walk back. In early April, days could have a springtime warmth and the nights a winter coldness, and on this morning the temperature was already past fifty.

On the corner of Myrtle and Clinton, they were stopped as a trolley and coal wagon passed. A dozen people stood around them, but Nolan noticed one man looking at him as if he knew him, a man who was recognizable to Nolan as well. Where had they met? Did he live on their street?

As he puzzled it out, the traffic cleared and the crowd began to cross. In Nolan's mind, the worlds of Brooklyn and Hell's Kitchen were not on the same planet, so it did not occur to him initially that the man was not from his Brooklyn neighborhood. When he did realize how he knew him, fear shot through him. He was one of the men arrested with Nolan at the Irish rally a month earlier. He was one of the Germans in the same cell and he knew Baumann.

Reaching the opposite corner, his heart racing, Nolan did not look back to see if the man was following. Hopefully, the chest on his shoulder had shielded his face enough to avoid recognition.

His heart was still pounding as they climbed the front steps of their building on Clinton Avenue. He still had not looked back. In the front hallway, as Sheenagh guided him, he quickly maneuvered the chest down the angular hallway to their apartment door at the far end.

She unlocked it and went in first, but as he navigated the chest through the door, his vision blocked, he heard the building's front door open behind him and the noise from the street spill in.

As rapidly as he could, he set down the chest inside and locked the door, even the extra, nighttime bolt lock.

"Can you bring it into the bedroom?"

"Just a second." Nolan stood very still, listening for any noise in the hallway. He heard the building door open then close then silence in the hallway as whoever it was seemed to have gone out again.

"John, I'm waiting. Can you bring it in?"

"Just a second."

She came to the bedroom door and watched him as he retrieved his revolver from the front room closet.

"What's going on?" she whispered.

"Just wait in the bedroom."

He went back to the apartment door and put his ear to the gap between the door and the frame. He still heard nothing. In a moment, though, the building door opened again and he heard the Shapiros, their upstairs neighbors, talking. He heard them open their mailbox in the foyer and discuss what was in the mail.

Nolan unlocked the door, keeping his revolver out of sight.

Mr. Shapiro turned. "John, you're home."

"For the day, yes."

"Tell Sheenagh hello," Mrs. Shapiro said. "And tell her I'll bring down the baby shoes later that I told her about."

He smiled, closed the door, and locked it again.

Sheenagh was standing behind him. "John, what was that about?"

He shook his head. "Nothing, I guess."

———❦———

An hour later, Nolan was drying the breakfast dishes in the kitchen while Sheenagh was in the front room, putting glasses in the sideboard. He heard what he thought was a cabinet door closing. It was not until he heard bolts unlocking that he realized it had been a knock at the door. He shouted her name as he ran from the kitchen but it was too late.

The German was standing in the doorway, his pistol drawn and pointing at Sheenagh. A short thin man, his face had a menacing confidence with the pistol in his hand.

He sneered at Nolan. "Are you John Nolan?" He had only a slight German accent.

"I'm … I'm not," Nolan said, reacting instinctively. "I'm James O'Connell. Who are you?"

"The mailbox says Mr. John Nolan, a private detective. I come in earlier and seen it. So I asks around the neighborhood. 'Who is this John Nolan?' They say he's a private detective what lives in the first-floor apartment. So that must be you."

Nolan shook his head. "This woman's husband is John Nolan but he's out of town. Like I said, my name's James O'Connell and I'm her cousin. I'm not friends with her husband, so I only visit her when he's gone. Why are you looking for him? What's he done to you? And please point your pistol away from this woman. She's done nothing. And can't you see? She's expecting a baby."

Sheenagh was shaking and near tears. The German hesitated, thought a bit, then turned the gun toward the sofa but held it steady.

"Where's her husband? Where'd he go to? When's he going to be back?"

"I know you from somewhere," Nolan said. "Do you know me?"

"Where do you live?"

"I live up in Hell's Kitchen."

The German seemed to be accepting the story and the gun barrel dipped down to the floor. "Yeah, I know you and you know me but I ain't going to say from where."

Now there were sounds of someone on the stairs in the hallway. It was Mrs. Shapiro, who had a pair of white baby shoes in her hand. The German turned and tried to hide the pistol but she saw it.

"Oh, my lord. What's going on here?"

"Who are you?" The German demanded.

"I'm their upstairs neighbor," she said with alarm.

The German raised the revolver again. "*Their* neighbor? This man lives here?"

"John, what's going —"

Before she could finish, Nolan jumped the startled German, grabbing the hand with the pistol and kicking his feet out from under him at the same time. The gun fired, but away from anyone, putting a bullet into the far wall. Both Sheenagh and Mrs. Shapiro screamed, but Nolan, significantly bigger than the German, was quickly able to get him pinned to the ground. At the same time, he twisted the pistol from the man's hand without it firing a second time.

"Go up to the Shapiro's apartment! But first go to the street and yell for a bluecoat!"

Once they were out of the apartment, Nolan kicked the door closed with a free leg.

"You're a detective, ain't you. You're this Nolan."

"Just shut up," Nolan said.

"Your bluecoat will get here and I'll be taken to jail and that'll be the end of you."

"Oh yeah? And how's that? You'll be the one in jail."

"How long do you think it'll take me to get your real

name and address to my friends? They'll hunt you down, you traitor. You're finished. Your wife? Your baby? That's the end of them too. Your pretty wife, imagine what someone like me is gonna do to her, you bastard, you stinking bastard!"

The German, on his back on the carpeted floor with Nolan sitting on his chest, spit at him. Nolan hit him in the face with the butt of the pistol, which stopped him from doing it again.

He had to think fast, though. This German *would* be able to get to his friends from his jail cell. There might even be German officers on duty in the jail who would pass along his information. It might be just a matter of hours before Baumann would know who Nolan was and where his family lived. Not only would his and Sheenagh's lives be in danger, but the investigation would be finished and the bombings might not be stopped.

Nolan felt a resolve just then, the kind of calm resolve he knew to trust. He had the man's pistol in his right hand. He searched his conscience for a sense of right or wrong about what he was about to do, but he continued to feel the same resolve.

Taking a deep breath, he swung the pistol over the man's open mouth, with the barrel angled up toward the top of his head, and fired instantly.

The bullet exited the back of his skull, putting a splatter of blood, bone fragments, and pink brain material on the carpet. The man's eyes never closed. They just took on a stunned, blank look.

Seconds later, Nolan heard shouting in the front hallway.

"Sheenagh, I'm all right!" Nolan yelled. "But go

upstairs with the Shapiros!"

"John, are you sure—"

"I'm fine, but please, stay upstairs. Let the police handle it."

—◆≈◆—

"Just give me your full name," said the patrolman.

"I can't," said Nolan. He sat on the sofa, feeling like he was about to vomit. Two other patrolmen were rolling the body into a oilskin sheet for transport outside to a patrol wagon. Several other patrolmen were milling about in the hallway.

"Listen, Paddy, give me your damn name or I'll arrest you for that too."

"I'm working undercover for the police department. Please, there's a telephone right there. I'll give you the number to call. Captain Thomas Tunney. He's the one —"

"Tunney of the bomb squad?"

"Yes, he hired me. I'm not in the police department but I work for him. I'm undercover and can't have my name in any police report or it will endanger what we're doing."

"You aren't on the force so why the hell would the department hire you? They have undercover men already."

"I'm not allowed to tell you."

The patrolmen frowned, seemed to believe little of it, but went to the telephone anyway. Nolan told him the number and the patrolmen gave it to the central operator and waited.

Nolan felt whatever was in his stomach start to rise into his throat. He stayed still and the feeling subsided. He thought at first that it was the result of the sickly smell left in the room by the blood and bits of bone and flesh. He realized, though, that it was more than that. He had killed a man. As much sense as pulling the trigger made, he had still killed a human being.

The patrolman finally shook his head and hung up.

"Tunney isn't answering. I need your full name and I better get it now."

—◆⟞⊰⟝◆—

Nolan sat by himself in a cold interrogation room at Brooklyn police headquarters for nearly forty minutes before someone came back in.

"Follow me."

He was taken to the office of the precinct commander. Tunney was there as well. As soon as Nolan came in, the commander left, leaving Nolan alone with Tunney.

"Your name's been dropped from any records," Tunney said. "And I have the incident report they wrote out. It says you and this German were struggling and his pistol went off accidentally. Only thing is the bullet went up into his mouth. How did that happen, John?"

Nolan took a deep breath. Then he told how he subdued the man, got his gun, how Sheenagh went to find a patrolman, and how the German's threatened to expose him and kill his family and ruin the investigation.

"I, uh … It didn't go off accidentally, sir."

Tunney sighed. "You know, this is the kind of thing we deal with all the time with our undercover agents. It would be years before he got out of jail. He wouldn't get to you."

"But if he was in jail, he could have gotten word to his friends. And they would have gotten to me. Besides, the whole investigation would have been wrecked and we'd lose the chance to stop these bombings."

Tunney considered this and then sighed heavily. "I guess you're right. I'm not going to fault you. But don't tell anyone else. All right? We'll let the story stand that it was an accidental shooting while you fought the man."

Nolan nodded. Tunney picked up his coat to leave, and Nolan, putting on his coat, glanced at the wall clock. He had to be in the Bronx in two hours to meet the German for the drive to Connecticut.

"Sir, I've learned something important," Nolan said. "The bombings are scheduled for Easter morning."

"Today's the eighth. That's, what, fifteen days."

"And this German who's come to New York – they're calling him the Easter man."

"The Easter man? Makes it sound like a children's book," Tunney shook his head as he buttoned his coat.

"One more thing, sir," Nolan said "I saw a newspaper-man outside my apartment as I was being taken out. I'm afraid this will get into the papers."

"I'll speak to the newspapers. Your name won't be mentioned. We'll say an unidentified robber got into the building and was wrestled to the ground by tenants in the front hallway and his gun went off."

"Into his mouth? Won't that sound suspicious?"

Tunney smiled. "I'll tell them the bullet ricocheted off a steam radiator and somehow got him in the mouth."

"We don't have steam radiators."

They settled on a metal umbrella stand.

❖

"Sheenagh, it wasn't my fault."

"I know." She was standing in the Shapiro's front room, crying. The Shapiros remained in the kitchen to give them privacy.

"But you're acting like it was."

"I'm not acting any way other than I'm upset, which I am and which anyone would expect me to be, seeing what I saw."

"We can clean the carpet."

"No. I want it thrown out. Even if you clean it, there'll be a stain. "

"A small one."

"You'd still see it. Always."

"Then we'll throw it out. Sheenagh, I have go. I have to drive up to —"

"To see a man's ... his ... his *brains* on your floor."

"I know."

"Can you understand how that makes me feel? In my home? In my —"

"It wasn't my fault."

"I know, but this man, he pointed a gun right at me, at your baby."

"And now he's dead. And in a month, I'll be an accountant again."

"I didn't come to America to have men with guns —"

"Sheenagh, please. It wasn't my fault."

He embraced her, half expecting her to pull away angrily, but instead she pushed into him softly. In silence they began to sway back and forth.

"Please, John," she whispered. "Just come back from this without getting your own brains spread onto someone's carpet. Can you promise me that?"

Aboard the fishing boat

32

The River Inspection

BECKER RENTED A motorized fishing boat for a four-hour excursion into the Hudson River from 53rd Street. Schwegel met him dockside.

With the boat still tied up, the captain and two mates were preparing the fishing rods, bait buckets, nets, and gaffs. Becker and Schwegel, onboard, stood by the side rail.

"Fellows," the captain called over. "You sure you want to stay only in the river? The fishing's better out beyond the harbor."

"Just cruise the river," Becker said. "We don't even know if we're going to fish. It's mainly a chance for my young friend to see the Manhattan skyline."

"You could have taken a cruise ship, sir. Quite a bit cheaper."

"We want to see certain things, and there's other things we don't care to see. I wrote it down for you."

The captain raised the sheet of paper. "Then do you fellows mind if my boys fish? They've got families."

"They can fish all they want. We don't even want any of what they catch." Becker leaned in to Schwegel. "You don't want to eat fish caught in this sewer trap anyway."

Once out on the Hudson, the captain was to make slow, repeated trips up and down the river. The lines were cast off and the boat cautiously backed into the current. Ferries, tugs, steamers, and sloops filled the river. The forecast called for a light rain, but any clouds that might produce it were yet to be seen. For the time being, the sun was warm.

"What are your impressions of New York so far?" Becker asked.

"It's ... different," Schwegel said.

"Have you been out much?"

"No. I'm worried I'll be recognized."

"You won't be. Not in New York. It's too big for anyone to know anyone. I'll tell you, I've been to London, to Paris, to Berlin of course, and New York is quite a revelation. It's not just the skyscrapers and the subways and all the modern things. It's the people. In Europe, you go to the theater and people point out this duke, that earl, that princess. The old families. Here, they point out the coal king, the wheat king, the bond king. It's money here that's important. And everyone here, from the poorest fellow up, feels they have a chance to make some. It gives this city a feeling of possibility you don't sense in Europe. Every place you walk here, people walk faster on the sidewalks because they're all going somewhere and they're all excited to get there."

Schwegel glanced over at him. "Are you German or American?"

Becker turned away, shaking his head.

"There's new things in London too," Schwegel said, "but I don't like the English any more for it."

"I didn't say I liked the Americans. I just —"

"I don't respect or like or admire Americans. They're stupid people, and they're our enemy until they speak up and say otherwise."

"I just mean there is a lot to … to notice about New York that's interesting."

"All I see is a dirty city."

"How far have you walked?"

"Around my neighborhood."

"Which is all warehouses and manufacturing buildings and that's all. You should walk up to Broadway, if you want to see the city."

Both men grew quiet. After a moment, Becker pointed at a freighter turning into a berth at 46th Street. "The *Sunset Rose*," He looked at a small notebook. "Departing April twenty-first. Going to Southampton. It will carry shells for certain but it will depart too soon for us. What do you know about the hulls on these ships? Will your bombs be enough?"

"The bombs have been tested."

"These ships – most have steel hulls now, up to an inch thick, thinner maybe toward the bow where there's less stress than in the middle."

"The bombs have been well tested in Berlin. I know the chemical ratios to use."

"My young friend, I'm trying to educate you to the reality of New York shipping."

Schwegel turned away. My young friend. If he had to hear that one more time. "What about the divers? Are they ready?"

"We're training men in Poughkeepsie," Becker said. "It's upstate on the Hudson. By Easter they'll be experts."

"How many?"

"You said you need ten teams to set the bombs."

"I've changed my mind. If we put ten boats into the river at the same time, that would be noticed. I need three efficient teams. On the night we set the bombs, one team will work the piers on the New Jersey side, one lower Manhattan, one the East River."

"You'll need to set the timers for different lengths. The teams will need a certain amount of time at each ship."

"I realize that, so we're going to have to make a practice run with one set of divers, to see how fast they can work and how much apart we'll have to set the timers for two different ships."

"When do you want this test?"

"Easter is twelve days from now. So the test should be within a week. Bring your best team down to the city and I'll find targets. Another thing. Your group, all these men you've assembled. I was told you think there's a spy in there somewhere. My God, Herr Becker, can't you do your job?"

"I ... I operate on the assumption that there's always a spy in a network somewhere. But yes, we're close to finding this one. I only give important information to the ones I trust, though. The others, I tell nothing to, except what they need to know that day to do their job, and I suspect he's one of those. This is my worry, though, not yours ... I want to say this again. I truly believe it's a mistake not to put bombs in Grand Central Terminal. I know you believe killing civilians is a mistake, but I believe we should set timed bombs on the tracks at least and possibly in Macy's when it's closed on Easter."

"No."

"Why, for God's sake?"

Schwegel turned and leveled a glare at Becker. How he despised this man, his thinly hidden condescension toward him, dripping from every sentence he spoke to him. Becker's words seemed to say, "Yes, you're in charge, but how utterly stupid was some German bureaucrat for picking you to lead this." And his smile, his fraudulent, deceitful smile accompanying every back-handed insult he delivered, as if his underlying opinion could be so easily disguised.

"I don't have to tell you why, Herr Becker, so I won't. From now on, just do what you're told."

"Well, I did, Herr McFee. I went to all the expense of training ten teams of divers as you asked and now you tell me, no, just three teams are needed. Yes, I did what I was told, Herr McFee, and how much has it cost our mission, this unnecessary training?"

"Conditions change. That's part of any mission."

"What conditions changed that made ten too many teams and three the right amount, Herr McFee?"

"My thinking changed."

"Yes, but conditions didn't. You just learned something I already knew, Herr McFee."

"I don't recall you telling me ten was too many, Herr Becker."

"I don't recall you letting me tell you anything, Herr McFee. You just seem to think you know it all, so you don't listen."

Schwegel did not respond, choosing to seethe in silence.

Hauxthausen with the acids

33

A Trip to Norwalk

EACH AFTERNOON, THE acids were waiting for them at the Hollweg Compressor Company in Norwalk. The tightly sealed bottles were placed on the back seat of Nolan's motor. Rather than carry both sulfuric and nitric acid in the same trip, he had decided to take only the sulfuric this trip, then the nitric the next. A sharp-eyed policeman might make the connection to TNT otherwise.

It was Sunday and this was their third afternoon picking up the acids. The day was clear but terribly cold. Without proper windows on Nolan's machine, a Dodge that Becker obtained for him, the driver's gloved hands would soon become stiff. Every fifteen miles or so, Nolan and his German partner, Hauxthausen, who said he had wrestled for Germany at the 1912 Olympics, would pull to the side of the road and trade places.

It was while Hauxthausen was driving on the nearly empty Boston Post Road near sunset in Connecticut that they were stopped by a police motorcar.

The officer got out of his machine carrying a night-stick and leading a fierce-looking, muzzled dog on a leash. He tapped the driver's door with the club. "You know why I stopped you?"

"No," Nolan said.

"You turned onto the parkway and didn't signal."

"You need that dog for something like a signal?"

"To be honest, I was tracking two convicts who escaped from Ossining and I thought maybe they stole a car and you were them. But both of them are older."

When the officer asked about the package on the back seat and heard Hauxthausen's German accent, he grew suspicious again. They were told to get out of the car and sit on the side of the road, on the edge of the weeds, while he examined the package.

With the noise of their engines gone and the parkway empty, the day had found its natural silence, broken only by the occasional call of a gull from Long Island Sound nearby.

"Sir," Nolan said. "Can I ask you not to open it? They're engraving acids. If the bottles should leak, it would ruin the seat fabric and the car isn't mine. It's my employer's."

"Is that so?"

"It would come out of my pay."

"Why don't you just be quiet and I'll tell you when I want to hear anything from you."

The officer was fumbling with the twine and paper covering the package. His muzzled dog was staring at Hauxthausen, who appeared angry that his suit might be getting dirty in the weeds. He leaned over to Nolan and whispered, "I can break this man's neck easy, if you want me to."

Nolan shook his head. "No. This may be nothing."

The officer managed to get the paper off the bottles. "Says here engraving acid, so maybe I'll believe you. What do you engrave?"

"Mostly athletic trophies," Nolan said. "It's sulfuric acid, which you don't want to get on you."

Seeming convinced of their story, he gently placed the two bottles back on the seat. "There's still the matter of the signaling. I could fine you for that, if I felt like it."

"Sir," Nolan said. "I could offer you something if it would make you feel you could let us keep driving. We've only got a few miles to go."

Nolan took a dollar bill out of his money clip and held it up. The officer eyed him with contempt but took the bill anyway. As Hauxthausen passed him to get back in their machine, without warning, he threw an arm around the officer's neck, a wrestling headlock, and twisted violently. Hearing the gruesome snap of the man's neck bone, Nolan cursed loudly and scrambled back into the driver's seat. The dog began barking wildly, almost coming out of its muzzle as it lunged at Hauxthausen.

"Damn it! Get in before someone comes by!"

However, another automobile could be seen approaching from behind.

"Don't drop him yet!" Nolan yelled. "Hold him like you're talking to him until this damned machine goes by."

Hauxthausen pretended to be talking to the officer as he held him up. "And how's you lovely wife, officer. And how's your lovely children, officer."

The machine went by without slowing.

"Put him in back of his motor, out of sight, and get in."

The dog was racing around the police motor, barking and straining at the muzzle. Hauxthausen kicked at it but missed as he ran back to their machine. Nolan quickly started it and the moment Hauxthausen was in he sped away, with the dog loudly barking.

"I told you not to do that!"

Hauxthausen was nearly laughing. "I enjoyed it."

"Idiot. Once we bribed him, there was no need."

"It felt good. He never knew what happened. He was dead the minute I done it."

They did not speak the rest of the way into the city, although periodically, Nolan would look over to see Hauxthausen smiling.

<hr />

"Sir, this is John." He was at the public phone in the Hotel Flanders.

"It's nearly midnight," Tunney said. "You're aware of that, I hope."

"Sorry to call you at home, but something happened."

Nolan told him about being stopped on the Pelham Parkway and what Hauxthausen had done.

"Well, you'll be surprised to hear the officer didn't die," Tunney said. "It was his collarbone what got broken. He passed out from shock, I guess. But a truck driver was passing and saw a dog in the middle of the road barking. He stopped and found the patrolman and took him to Fordham Hospital. When I heard about the acids and the German, though, I wondered if you might be involved, so I kept it out of the newspapers for now."

Nolan felt a wave of relief. "There's another thing.

When we dropped off the bottles, I was told there's a meeting at the cold storage locker on 35th Street in the morning and I have to go to it. This man didn't know what it was about. All he knew was that he was told to give me the message that I was required to be there."

"So?"

"It's just … this business about the traitor. Maybe they've figured out I'm him."

"I see. So you think this could be to assassinate you."

"I don't think so, but there's a chance." They both were silent for a moment. "The problem is if I don't go, or if you rush in to save me and arrest these men when the meeting starts, the chance to stop these bombings will be lost. And they'll probably go on anyway. The Germans will just bring in new men to work with this bombmaker, this specialist, and we still don't know who he is. But I might be wrong about what this meeting is about. I probably am. It probably has nothing to do with any traitor. What I'm saying is I should go."

He heard Tunney sigh on his end. "All right. I'll have my men in a bakery truck on 35th. But if you don't come out, we'll arrest these men."

"One thing. If something happens, my wife —"

"I'll figure out a way to take care of her, I promise. But, John, make it out alive somehow."

"I plan to. I'll take precautions. I promise."

Becker's bodyguard

34

The Traitor Revealed

A S HE ENTERED the building, Nolan saw the police bakery truck parked across the street. The meeting, as before, was in an empty cold storage locker on the second floor.

Sitting outside the room was a bodyguard, who stood as Nolan approached and gestured that he stop to be frisked. Instantly, Nolan noticed how much taller the man was than himself.

The revolver in his shoulder holster was taken, but the small knife Nolan hid in one boot and the two-shot pocket pistol in the other were not found.

Inside, still lacking ice, the room had grown even more hot and dank. The lighting was not good, which favored him. A half dozen folding chairs were set out and three gray-haired men were already seated, but Becker was not there yet.

"Does anyone know what this is about?" Nolan asked.

"Herr Becker called it. We don't know."

In a moment, Becker arrived and he brought the bodyguard into the room then bolted the door behind them. Nolan's heart began to race. In previous meetings, the bodyguard had always stayed outside. Nolan checked his boot to make sure the pistol, his first line of defense, could be easily reached.

Becker and the three other men were all past sixty and would likely be easy to handle. So it was the bodyguard he had to take. With the first mention of Nolan as a traitor, he would have to shoot him and hopefully be able to stop the other men before they had a chance to get to him. Two shots and a knife. Would that be enough?

Becker did not immediately sit, taking out a handkerchief to wipe his glasses. The three older Germans fidgeted in their chairs.

"Herr Becker," one of them said. "This meeting — What's it for?"

Becker cleared his throat, seeming to do it for dramatic effect. "The spy in our group," he said. "We finally know who it is."

Nolan's fingers curled around the pistol grip. The bodyguard had settled into the chair opposite him and was unbuttoning his jacket, looking relaxed. Hopefully, he would be unprepared for what was about to happen.

"What spy? I never heard this," one of the older Germans said.

"I didn't tell everybody. We found out there was a spy working for us."

Nolan's index finger found the trigger. This was probably the moment, before he was accused, when the element of surprise would be on his side. He leaned forward slightly, setting himself.

"I want you all to think," Becker said. "A man named Fuchs. Do you remember him? Tall? A thin mustache? About thirty? If you remember him, can you recall anything you told him?"

Confused, Nolan loosened his fingers momentarily.

"Fuchs? Anyone? No? Well, he was the spy. But he's dead now."

Becker told the story. Fuchs, whose real name was Linley, grew up in Germany because his father was a diplomat in the British Consulate in Berlin. The boy later went home to England and became part of British intelligence when the war broke out.

"We found out who he was and gave him bad information to transmit to the British. Then last night, after we made sure he'd passed it, we shot him."

The rest of the meeting was about a mission to recruit more Irishmen for work after the Easter bombings, for a new round of bombings to keep the pressure on the Americans.

However, out of danger, Nolan was light-headed, barely able to follow what Becker was saying. He realized that somewhere in the back of his mind, he had expected that by this point in the meeting he might be dead or be trying to kill others to stay alive.

"And Herr Sweeney," Becker said. "The Irish mission – that's one I'd like you to lead. I'll contact you in the next few days about it."

The ferry to New Jersey

35

The *Reliance* Goes Down

O N SUNDAY EVENING, at eight minutes to midnight, the two divers, dressed in rubberized suits, got in a rowboat beneath the pier at 49th street. It had been left for them by Becker earlier in the day.

In the shadows of the pier and its pilings, where no light reached, Schwegel handed them the first bomb, a metal canister the size of a milk bottle.

"Make sure the magnets go against the hull," he said. "Otherwise, it'll fall right to the bottom. That's the real bomb. This second one ... here... it's the empty casing and has a 'two' on it. Use the watch I gave you and write down the exact time each one is set in place. And if there are any irregularities, such as if you're delayed getting to the second ship, write that down."

The men nodded and carefully put the bombs under a blanket, where they also had a revolver and their diving masks.

Their targets were the ferry *Reliance*, berthed at the 42nd Street pier, and a freighter, *The India Light*, berthed at 39th Street. The plan was to test one real bomb, the one that would go on the *Reliance*, to make sure the explosion, which was timed to go off in twelve hours, would punch through the hull, and to measure the elapsed time to attach the empty bomb casing to *The India Light*. If both bombs were real, the two explosions would surely alert authorities to sabotage. If only the ferry went down, the cause would be debated. A boiler explosion perhaps?

Using his foot, Schwegel pushed the rowboat off the gravel shore and away from the pilings until it floated into the slow current of the Hudson.

The bomb on the *Reliance* was set to go off at fifteen minutes past noon the next day, Monday, April seventeenth, six days before Easter, when the ferry would be well into the Hudson on a scheduled crossing to New Jersey.

By noon, Schwegel, Becker, and two representatives of the German Consulate in New York who were there to witness the test, had walked west on 42nd Street to the pier's entry ramp. The *Reliance* was just making its departure from the berth, its deck filled with people, when they reached the pier. Schwegel guessed the ferry was carrying nearly five hundred passengers.

The day was sunny and unusually warm for mid-April. In anticipation of Easter, many on deck had optimistically left their coats at home and were smiling as they drank in the sunlight.

Schwegel, walking with a man named Brandt, a former military officer and now a special envoy attached to the Consulate in New York City, slowed slightly to allow Becker and his German to move a distance ahead.

"Herr Brandt, can I make a request?"

Brandt, apparently sensing something confidential

was about to be said, stopped on the sidewalk.

"I'd like to ask a slight change in the people involved with this mission," Schwegel said.

"That isn't a problem," Brandt said.

"I'd like Becker gone."

"I thought —"

"You asked earlier how we were getting along, and I had to say things were fine because he was standing right there. But things are not fine. He's very difficult to work with."

The two men looked out onto the river as the *Reliance* moved fully into the river current.

Brandt was frowning. "Herr Becker has been working for us in New York for several years. He's done —"

"I know that and that's the problem. He resents that Berlin chose me instead of him and that —"

"Let me finish. He's done an exemplary job for us. He's very loyal and very capable. He's valuable."

"But isn't this mission crucial?"

"Of course it is."

"Then I want him gone. It's six days until Easter. At this critical moment, his uncooperative attitude could ruin this mission. Move him to another city. I'm sure there are missions there he could lead."

"If I move him, he'll see it as an insult. New York is our most important target. He knows that."

"I don't care. I want him gone."

Becker, up ahead, glanced back at them. Schwegel could see suspicion in his expression.

"Just so you know," Brandt said. "Herr Becker has told me he thinks you're doing a poor job leading this mission."

"He told you that?"

"Several times."

"Now that I know that, I want him gone immediately."

"I can't do that. Berlin wants him here."

"Berlin chose me to lead this mission. They didn't assign it to Becker and there's a good reason. He doesn't know anything about the explosives and devices that will work in a marine situation like this. I do. Only I can build these bombs."

"Becker is —"

"Becker is a fool."

"I know him well and he's anything but a fool."

Schwegel glared at Brandt. "Can Becker build you these bombs? No, he can't."

Brandt looked at the *Reliance*. "Will your bombs even work, Herr McFee? Isn't that the first question to be answered?"

Schwegel was silenced by this. He looked at his pocket watch. Eleven minutes past noon.

Sunlight glinting off its railings, the *Reliance* moved steadily across the slow-moving river, which widened to nearly a mile and half as it passed central Manhattan on its way to the harbor and ocean. A gasoline freight boat crossed in front of it, bringing a short blast of the ferry's horn.

The shrill answering whistle of the freight boat nearly drowned out the sharp crack of the bomb exploding. Well below the water line, the detonation was also muffled by the depth of water. However, a violent shake of the ferry and the belch of smoke that bubbled up from beneath its hull on the port side said the bomb had done its job.

Schwegel, feeling the thrill of vindication, rushed to the pier fence as did Brandt.

Men scrambled on the ferry's lower deck, a crowd of both passengers and ferrymen rushing to the rail to investigate. About a hundred yards into the channel, the ferry began tipping noticeably to that side, either from the weight of people shifting to it or the sudden intake of water into the hull.

The ferry's captain began sounding the horn repeatedly to signal trouble. One long blast followed by two short ones. At the pier, those waiting for the next ferry at first seemed only mildly curious about what was going on. Surely, it was nothing serious. The ferry hit a log in the current possibly or someone fell overboard.

The listing of the *Reliance* quickly became obvious, though. On shore, the yelling started. "Get smaller boats out there! Get tugs to the ship!"

The engine of the *Reliance* was still operating at full throttle although the motor seemed to be struggling. Schwegel guessed the captain would to try to return to the pier before the ship sank. However, the motor died, perhaps from being flooded. Quickly, the ship was sideways in the current.

The railing on the port side was nearly into the water. Passengers were panicking and a man jumped overboard. A tug finally reached the ferry and crowds of people moved to the stern to board it, overwhelming the balance even more. As the ferry took water over the deck rail, more men jumped into the water, likely near freezing at this time of year despite the warmth of the day. A woman carrying her child jumped, then, pushed by the crowd, several men went over the rail.

Brandt pointed to a cameraman rushing onto the pier. "The newsmen are here. We can't be photographed. Let's walk down the river."

Their pace along the sidewalk was about as fast as the current of the Hudson. Schwegel glanced back. The ferry was sinking fast. However, the bodies of the first to go over the side were staying even with them as they walked. Several appeared dead already. Schwegel guessed many who took the ferry did not know how to swim. One, a man still wearing his derby, was weakly waving his arms and calling for help. A motorized fishing launch was trying to reach him.

"Congratulations, Herr McFee. Your bomb was exact down to the minute. Won't this be a spectacle on Easter. All that noise and smoke."

"It won't be," Schwegel said.

"What does that mean?"

"These explosions won't be heard and there will barely be any smoke. I knew there wouldn't be."

"What do you mean you knew? Every time I heard about this plan, it was the idea that all of New York could come to a dead stop as dozens of explosions went off in the harbor and great plumes of smoke rose above the city."

"You never heard that from me. And if I told those bureaucrats in Berlin that the explosions were going to be too far below water to be heard, would they have ordered it? No. So I kept quiet."

"I thought the targets were going to be munitions ships. Wouldn't they —"

"Explode? Not unless the bomb sat right under a barrel of powder. These charges are only enough to blow a hole in the steel hull and sink them. You'd have to be lucky to set off the munitions."

Brandt looked puzzled. "But what's the point of only sinking these ships?"

Schwegel turned on him sharply. "New Yorkers might not hear the explosions or see smoke, but the next morning, what will they read about in the papers? What will be the headlines? Germans sabotage forty ships carrying munitions. That sends exactly the message to America we want. Stay out of the war. *That* is the purpose, not spectacle."

They had reached the 36th Street pier where the gate was open, so they walked onto it, joining a growing crowd. Bodies were drifting closer to the Manhattan side of the river, some face down in the current. One, that of a young woman, her face upturned, blue and lifeless, drifted close enough to the pier that a longshoreman, having climbed down on the ladder, tried to reach it with a pole hook but missed in two attempts.

"Herr Brandt. What about my request? What about Becker?"

"I'll try," Brandt said.

"Try?"

"All right," Brandt said. "We'll transfer Becker, but it will take a few days."

Schwegel was watching the young woman who kept drifting toward the harbor mouth and the ocean beyond. Her body joined with other lifeless bodies to create a raft of bodies, like a raft of sea kelp on the current. It was so eerie it made him smile.

———※———

On his way back to the basement laboratory, Schwegel stopped at a German market on West 37th street and bought fresh sauerkraut and rouladen for dinner. Standing at the counter, waiting his turn, he closed his eyes and breathed in the comforting and familiar smells so reminiscent of home, of Austria.

Locked in the laboratory again, he opened a bottle of wine and spread the feast on a work table. However, he had to struggle to get the lid off a jar of pickle relish. He took a seat and carefully studied the lid to determine why, treating it like an engineering problem.

How odd, he thought. He realized the sinking of the ferry was already vanishing from his thoughts, the sight of the bodies in the Hudson already disappearing from memory.

There was a phrase his mother would use when he was little. *"große Dinge werden schließlich kleine Dinge."* Big things eventually become small things. He never understood what she meant at that age, but he suddenly did. Death was a very big thing. Now it had been reduced to only a minor thing. In war, one could kill dozens of people one moment and study the stuck lid of a relish jar the next and feel almost nothing about those deaths. How very odd.

The office of the German Consulate

36

New Man in Charge

NOLAN HAD NOT heard from Becker since the meeting in the cold storage locker a week earlier. Becker said he would contact him and he never had.

With time running out – Easter was three days away – Nolan went to the office of the German Consulate on lower Broadway in hopes of finding him.

He waited on the sidewalk outside the building a half hour, but it was Herr Voigt he encountered, not Becker.

Voigt gestured that they not speak for the moment, indicating they should walk across the street to Bowling Green Park for privacy. Past the iron fence, they took seats on a bench near the statue of Abraham de Peyster. Nearby, a wedding party was posing for photographs by the circular fountain, the bride and her maids dressed in pink and carrying pink parasols.

"Herr Becker has been transferred out of New York," Voigt said with his strong German accent. "So you'll report to me from now on."

"Why was he moved? I thought he was doing a good job."

"No one cares vat you tink, Mr. Sweeney."

There was an undeniable edge to this. Nolan had to think. A new man in charge, showing that he was in charge. "I just asked. I meant nothing."

"Just do vat you're told. Don't misunderstand me. We appreciate da work you've done for da Fahderland, but ve vant men who accept dat da men in charge, which is now me, know vat dey're doing. Ve need men to follow orders."

"Easter is Sunday. What can I do to help?"

"Nutting. I got all da men I need for da moment. Ve'll contact you ven it's done. Do you need money? Let me see vat I got wit me." He quickly searched his pockets. "Forty dollars? Vould dat help."

Nolan took it. "But there must be something I can do before Sunday."

"Vat did I just say? Just do vat you're told. If I needed your help, I vould have said so."

Abruptly, Voigt rose to leave. Nolan stayed and as he tried to think, he watched Voigt stride officiously across Broadway for the Consulate. What do I do now?

<hr />

"Sir, this is John." He was at a public phone in the Knickerbocker Hotel

"Good. What do you have for me?" Tunney said.

"The Germans don't plan to use me anymore until after the bombings. I'm sorry. I've failed."

"Not yet. There are more men than you working on this, so if this fails, we've all failed. If you're not under-cover anymore, maybe we can arrest the few Germans you know about – this Becker you've mentioned, a few others – then we'll see what we can get out of them."

"Becker is gone and I'm not sure of the real names of the others I know. Everyone used aliases. We could arrest them, but most of these men don't know anything other than their own orders. That's the way they set up this spy ring. So we still might not find out who this Easter man is or where he is."

"Well, come into headquarters for a meeting tomorrow at ten and we'll figure it out."

"Sorry, sir."

"Stop apologizing, John. You have nothing to apologize for."

Tunney and his detectives sweat the suspect

37

The Package

G OOD FRIDAY IN Manhattan was expected to be overcast and rainy. Nevertheless, by nine o'clock crowds were already forming outside Trinity Church on lower Broadway for the noon service. Florists and bakeries throughout the city were busy with deliveries of Easter lilies and hot cross buns. And dress shops were doing a swift business in advance of Sunday's Easter Parade when women would wear their finest clothes in a massive procession up and down Fifth Avenue.

Nolan traveled downtown to Tunney's office. Without his usual wig and glasses, he was stopped at the front desk by the suspicious sergeant until he remembered the glasses were still in his overcoat pocket. Putting them on, he was waved upstairs.

He got to the conference room and took a seat as Tunney was passing out newspaper articles about the ferry sinking to Adcock and Michaels.

One of Tunney's detectives came to the conference

room door behind him and Tunney stepped outside with
the man for only a moment.

"About a half hour ago," he said when he returned,
"one of the express offices in the city called us. They've
been getting frequent shipments from a watchmaker in
Philadelphia and they got a new one last night. The
packages come into the office general delivery and
someone picks them up. So the detective who took the
call went over to check on it. Let's hope this turns out to
be something. It's two days until Easter and we're running out of time."

"Well, I have news, important news," Adcock said.
"I've found out that your man here is probably being used
as a decoy to give us misleading information. I was in
touch with British intelligence people and they also have
a man undercover and he's learned the actual target of
all these bombings will be the rail lines coming into New
York from New England. They're used by the freight
trains carrying shells and explosives to the docks. So I
plan to call the secretary in Washington this afternoon
and make a strong case why I should take over this ——"

Tunney put up a hand. "Stop right there, Adcock.
Don't make that call unless you want to look like a fool.
We already know about this information and it was the
bad information the Germans wantd us to have. I spoke
to your boss this morning. The man who passed it along
was fed it deliberately."

"Why wasn't I told this earlier?"

"You're being told right now. John only found out
about it last week and told me and I told the secretary
and now I'm telling you."

"How do you know John isn't the true decoy?"

"He was in a meeting with the Germans when they talked about how they uncovered the British agent's identity and how they gave him bad information so he would tell his British bosses. Then, after they were sure he'd passed it along, they shot him. We found the agent dead in his motor on the side of the road to Tarrytown two days ago, a bullet in his head."

"I still say he might have had the good information and your man is the decoy."

"Common sense says the Germans are after the freighters," Tunney said. "If they're sunk at sea, the munitions are lost. If the Germans blow up a rail line, they know we'll get the cargo to New York some other way."

Adcock started to raise another argument of protest but then seemed to realize the futility.

"About this ferry," Tunney said. "We haven't told the newspapers what we found yet. The *Times* figured the steam boiler exploded. The *Herald* took a guess that maybe it was carrying a freight truck with a box of dynamite on it that might have gone off accidentally. But we think it was a bomb attached to the outside of the hull."

"Why do you think that?" Adcock asked.

"The hole it left," Tunney said. "The metal around the edge was pushed in, not out."

"Sir, the Robert Fay case," Nolan said. "Wasn't his bomb supposed to attach to the hull at the rudder? Maybe they've brought that plan back."

"I thought of that," Tunney said. "But this hole wasn't anywhere near the rudder."

"But a ferry," Adcock said. "What's the point of sinking a harmless ferry? Fifty-four people drowned."

"That we don't know."

"Maybe a German U-boat did it," Nolan said.

"It wouldn't go into the river," Tunney said. "They'd be too worried about the depth and trying to turn around. Besides, we keep putting out reports of Edison working on something to detect them in the river."

Adcock stood, his agitatiion growing. "How can you plant forty bombs on the hulls of ships and not get seen doing it? No. They'll blow up places like Macy's, places where a lot of people will die. I know these Germans. They're vicious. This ferry proved it."

"How can they set forty bombs at busy places like department stores around the city and not get seen?" Michaels asked. "Macy's is crowded in the day and well guarded at night."

This drew a glare from Adcock.

"You have to think of what drives the Germans," Nolan said. "Mainly, they want to keep America out of the war. That's what obsesses them. If they blow up Macy's and kill hundreds of people, what's going to be the reaction? We'd declare war the next day. I'm sure it'll be munitions ships in the harbor."

Adcock vehemently shook his head. "What about this ferry? More than fifty people died. Has anyone declared war?"

"No one has proof yet that the Germans did it," Nolan said.

"You're wrong. Americans won't ever join this war, no matter what happens," Adcock said. "Americans are a lazy people. Americans want to go motoring and tend their gardens and read their magazines and go out to the ball park to see the Senators play. You wouldn't get enough boys to sign up to fight if we did declare war."

Nolan shook his head. "One bomb at Macy's is all it would take."

Adcock scowled. "It's idiotic to think —"

"Stop it." Tunney said. "We've got other business and we're losing time." He examined his notes. "The department is putting on three hundred extra police reserves to patrol the harbor and downtown starting Saturday afternoon. Something else. We've still got our tap going in Rutherford, so Adcock, there's something we want you to leak to the Germans." He slid a paper across the conference table to him. "This is what I want you to say in a call tonight. It's about J. P. Morgan. Right now, almost single-handedly, he's funding the Allies, giving them loans to pay for this fight."

Adcock sat and read the script out loud. "We think J. P. Morgan is their only target right now. So we will be using most of our men to guard him." He looked up. "That's what you want me to say?"

"Yes," Tunney said. "We think that will convince them to leave Morgan alone. Just so you know, this isn't my idea. It came from higher up."

"From Morgan I'll bet," Adcock said.

"No, from your boss. From Secretary McAdoo."

This worried Adcock. "Does he know about this tap on my line?"

"Yes, he does."

"Does he know, well, how this … how it got discovered?"

"No, he doesn't," Tunney said. "I just told him we found a way to use a tap the Germans have on a particular line we know about. I didn't tell him yet it's your line."

Adcock reread the script, but he was clearly thinking

about something else.

"Can I make a request?" he asked. "Eventually, it will go into a report of how we used this German tap to feed them bad information. Can I request that we say that it was intentional to let my phone in Rutherford be tapped, that we made it known to the Germans that I was staying out there so they would tap it?"

"I might be able to do that," Tunney said. "But Adcock, if I agree to this, I don't want to hear that you're running around claiming it was your idea, that you saved this investigation all by yourself. We'll say it was Nolan's idea."

"Sir, we agreed my name would never be used in any official report. What about if we say it was Michaels' idea? In fact, it was his idea."

They all looked at Michaels.

"All right with me," Tunney said. "All right with you, Adcock?"

"I … well … I suppose so."

Tunney clapped Michaels on the back. "Congratulations, Michaels. Good work."

Now there was a knock on the door and they all turned. It was one of Tunney's detectives.

"Captain, we got the German who picked up the package. It was a clock altered to be a timer that you could use on a bomb. He's down in the first-floor interrogation room."

—◆—❊—◆—

"Then why did you pick up the parcel if it wasn't yours?"

Nolan, Michaels, and Adcock stood just outside the interrogation room listening but out of sight. Tunney and two of his detectives were inside with the door open. They were all shooting questions at the man. Nolan peeked in quickly and saw them standing threateningly around the German who was seated with his back to Nolan.

"A man paid me two bits to pick it up. I don't know his name. Big fella."

"Why didn't you have two bits on you when we brought you in?"

"I spent it."

"When?"

"Before I went in to the express office. I got breakfast first."

"While this big man waited for you to come back with the package, you went and got breakfast? Come up with better lies than that. Where were you taking it?"

"I ain't saying nothing else."

Nolan heard flesh being slapped.

"I still ain't saying nothing. I know my rights. All I did was pick up a clock."

"You said it wasn't your package. How did you know it was a clock?"

"The man I picked it up for told me it was a clock. I told him he had to tell me what was in it so's I knew I wasn't committing no crime. What's the crime in picking up a clock? Tell me that."

The suspect refused to answer anything else. Tunney came out of the interrogation room and everyone moved farther down the hallway to talk.

"John, you were an accountant. Right?"

He nodded.

"Then why don't you and Michaels take a train down

to Philadelphia. I'll call the police there and get you a search warrant for this watchmaker. If he was making regular shipments, maybe he was getting regular payments for them. Go through his books and see what you can find."

Bergmann at his workbench

38

The Watchmaker

THEY PULLED INTO the Broad Street Station before noon. They were met by a Philadelphia detective with a warrant based on probable cause of conspiracy and manufacturing bombs.

The watchmaker, Henry Bergmann, had a shop on Snyder Avenue. When the Philadelphia detective showed his badge and the warrant, Bergmann calmly sat on his stool at his workbench and returned to taking apart the very same kind of clock used for the timer. Michaels, seeming astonished by this, did not confiscate it right away. He stood by and watched while Nolan went through the man's accounting ledgers in the back office.

Under income, Nolan found repeated entries in recent months for fifteen dollars next to the initials LBF. He looked through the unopened mail for checks, but found nothing related to an LBF. He was looking through other files when he thought to look through a bank deposit bag on the edge of Bergmann's desk. Among the dozen or so checks was one for fifteen dollars signed by Louis B. Fischer, National City Bank of New York.

As it turned out, while Nolan was going through the books, two people came in to the store to place bets on the daily number with Bergmann. A search turned up blank betting slips and a record book of names, bets, and payoffs.

Bergmann was arrested for bookmaking, but the Philadelphia detective dropped off Nolan and Michaels at the train station before taking him in.

They were back in New York before three o'clock. A call to the National City Bank and a quick search of the records found that Louis B. Fischer Sr. had a metalworks and tin stamping business on West 38th Street in Manhattan.

After reporting to Tunney and quickly obtaining a fresh warrant, Michaels and four of Tunney's detectives prepared to take a police motor up to West 38th.

"Sir, I'd like to go with them," Nolan said.

"No, someone there might recognize you," Tunney said.

"What does it matter now? If they do recognize me, maybe they'll get worried enough that a police agent was in the ring that they'll cancel the bombings."

Tunney had to think about this. He turned to Michaels. "What do you think?"

"Actually, it makes sense."

<hr />

Eastern Metal Works Inc., a three-story building, took up most of the block. As Tunney's detectives showed their badges and the warrant to the guard in the front hallway, Nolan looked past them to the main work floor. It was filled with men busily working at drills, grinders, lathes, saws, and stamping machines.

They found Fischer in his office on the second floor. He did not seem surprised they were there. Evidently, the guard had called up to warn him.

"Who're you?"

"Police," Michaels said, handing him the warrant. "We want to ask you some questions and look around."

Fischer, gray-haired and portly, did not budge from his chair. "What questions?"

Michaels produced the check written to Bergmann. "What was this for?"

"How should I know?"

"You wrote dozens to him like this."

Fischer hesitated. "Oh, I remember. He was collecting for the German war widows fund. I felt compelled to give him something."

"We already arrested Bergmann. We know it wasn't for war widows. "

"That's what he told me it was for. The war widows. How was I supposed to know it wasn't."

Michaels gestured to Nolan to step outside the office for a moment. "Maybe the clocks were brought here," Michaels said. "Why don't I keep questioning Fischer, and you and the detectives look around."

They searched separate floors as the employees, mostly young men who eyed them suspiciously, kept working.

On the noisy first floor, after spending twenty minutes walking the aisles between machines and opening boxes and drawers, Nolan approached a worker. Over the noise of his band saw, Nolan asked him if there was a basement. He pointed to a metal fire door next to the floor foreman's office. As Nolan walked over, the foreman, a huge man in a pressed suit that said he never did any dirty work on the machines, came to the door.

"Who're you?"

"Police. I want to look in the basement. Fischer has our warrant."

"I need to check this with him." He returned to the office, made a telephone call, then came back.

"You want to look down there, go ahead, but it's just the furnace and coal storage. Fischer says I'm supposed to go down with you."

"I'll look myself."

"Fischer says no."

"We're the police. He isn't. Mind your own damn business and stay right there."

The foreman's lip curled, and for a moment, he looked like he was might charge Nolan, who began to reach for his holstered revolver inside his jacket. However, the foreman appeared to think better of it and returned to his office.

Nolan's suspicions raised, he ventured down the stairs, his revolver drawn. He found a light switch at the top that only lit a single bare bulb at the bottom of the steps. It was enough light to see that there was not much to see. The furnace system and a coal bin and little else.

Upstairs, he found Michaels waiting for him outside the floor foreman's office.

"Anything?" Michaels asked.

Nolan shook his head.

"Fischer is sticking to his story," Michaels said. "Hopefully, they can sweat the man who picked up the clocks for something."

Outside the building, they separated. Michaels and

the four detectives went back downtown. Nolan wanted to go back to his apartment on West 49th Street for a meal. However, as he started to leave, he looked back at Fischer's building. He realized the machine floor was a lot larger than the basement he had seen.

Curious, he walked down the narrow alley along the side of the building. Moving trash cans and shipping pallets, he could see small basement windows along its entire length. Past a certain point, though, the windows were blackened with paint.

Getting down on his knees at one of the blackened windows, he could see light through a thin sliver of the window glass that the paint had missed toward the top. He moved to another window and saw the same thing. A bright light, brighter than the bare bulb on the basement stairs could have produced.

As he started to rise, he felt something in his back and knew immediately it was a gun.

"You do vat I say or I don't mind shooting you right here." The voice had a German accent.

The man had him walk several feet ahead of him farther down the alley to a loading dock and an entry door.

"You knock and do it loud so dey can hear," he said.

Before Nolan knocked, he finally had a chance to glance back at the man. Perhaps twenty, dressed in a rumpled suit that was too large for him and holding the pistol with both hands on the grip as if he were inexperienced using it. The weapon had a silencer on its barrel. He was also inexperienced enough that he had not searched Nolan for a gun.

Nolan had to pound twice before the door opened. Another man, no older than the other, also in a suit and holding a revolver, stuck out his head.

"I seen him looking in da windows of da basement," The first man said. "Vat do we do wit him?"

They motioned Nolan inside. It was a shipping area with stacks of wooden pallets, empty barrels, and flattened cardboard boxes ready for the trash. The lighting was poor and the noise from the machinery in the next room was nearly deafening.

"I think he was one of the police detectives here to talk to Fischer," the second man said with barely a German accent. "This isn't good. Wait here. I'll go get Becker. Check this man for a gun."

"Becker got transferred to Chicago I tink," the first man said. "Da man in charge is da man who lives in da basement. I don't know his name."

With the point of his pistol, the first man motioned that Nolan should sit on one of the stacks of pallets. The machines inside thrummed and clattered and pounded. Keeping his pistol leveled at him, he roughly patted Nolan's waist for a weapon. Then he moved to his bulky overcoat, first patting the right side where most shoulder holsters would be. However, Nolan was left-handed, and the man only lightly patted the left side of the coat where the holster actually was, missing the Smith & Wesson.

"I'm not a policeman," Nolan said. "I'm only an accountant they brought along to look at Fischer's books."

"Shut up," the German said with a sneer, but he apparently believed him and quit searching for a weapon.

As they waited for the other German to return, Nolan slowly edged his foot sideways until the toe of his boot touched a tin cleaning bucket by the pallets. Waiting a few moments, with the drone of the machines distracting his captor, Nolan suddenly kicked the bucket across the cement floor, startling the German who jumped backward and nearly fell over one of the other stack of pallets. Nolan dove behind his stack and drew his revolver.

The German got his feet steady and began firing, with one shot narrowly missing Nolan and lodging in the plaster wall just behind his shoulder. Nolan fired back once, sending the German diving for cover. The shots were nearly drowned out by the constant noise from the machine room next door.

In the momentary standoff, Nolan saw there was a wooden door behind him. Unsure how many bullets he had left, he threw it open and crawled through and shut it, hoping he had found an escape. Instead, he found himself in a large darkened closet.

Seconds later, he heard voices outside. The second German had apparently returned.

Feeling about, he discovered the closet was almost a small room but with no windows or lights he could detect. Fearful they would start shooting through the door, he felt his way until he found a corner shielded by a discarded piece of machinery and several metal garbage cans. Sure enough, they started firing through the door, with splinters of wood flying about and bullets striking walls and metal cans but missing him.

Once the shots ended, Nolan fired back once through the door. "You didn't get me. You can see I've got a gun too and plenty of bullets. So I can sit here all day."

Short of breath, his heart pounding, he rolled open the cartridge cylinder and ran his finger over the chambers.

He had only one bullet left.

The finished bombs

39

Change of Plans

SCHWEGEL WAS FURIOUS. He paced the laboratory, trying to think. He had slowly gotten used to the faint smell of sulfuric acid in the air, but at the moment, it annoyed him terribly. He put a handkerchief to his nose.

The owner of the factory, Fischer, waited for his response.

"What do we do?" Fischer asked again. "The police knew timers were in the packages and they came to me, so they know —"

"They didn't know about the lab down here, correct?"

"They didn't seem to. They searched but missed it. Don't you think they might come back?"

Schwegel sighed. Of course, they will, you fool. If they know about the timers and they know their link to your factory, obviously they will come back.

He examined one of the finished bombs. All forty, in waterproof steel canisters fashioned upstairs, were standing in groups on the long work table. Paper tags were attached to each detailing the targets.

The North Dakota, 12:00, Pier 60, Chelsea docks
The Shenandoah, 12:14, Morris Canal pier, New Jersey
The Cedarwood, 12:33, Pier 38, South Brooklyn

Now there were two sharp knocks, a pause, then a softer knock on the lab's entry door, the code Schwegel had devised.

"What?" he yelled.

"More trouble, sir."

He unbolted the door. The second German came in.

"A policeman who came to see Herr Fischer. He came back. We got him caught in a storage closet. He's got a gun, though, and has been shooting back so we can't go in. What do we do?"

Schwegel leaned over and put his hands on his knees and took heavy breaths. The incompetence. "I'll go."

Led upstairs to the shipping area and shown the storage closet, Schwegel stepped away and thought. Fischer joined them.

"What's stored in there?" Schwegel asked him.

"Nothing important," Fischer said. "We keep empty trash cans in there, a few broken pieces of equipment. But there's no windows, no way out."

Schwegel stood silently as he thought, the eyes of the other men on him.

"Push those stacks of pallets in front of the door," he

said. "Just let him sit in there for now. One of you stay here and guard the door, but every once in a while, put another bullet into the door to remind him, but use your silencers so it can't be heard. We'll kill him tonight after the packages are gone."

"The bombs are going out tonight?" the second German asked.

Schwegel swung his arm to slap him, but the German ducked out of the way. Schwegel pointed to the door. "You idiot. He'll hear."

He motioned that they move to the side of the room and in whispers he informed them of the change.

"We're planting the bombs tonight so they explode at noon tomorrow," he said. "It's no difference if they go off Holy Saturday or Easter morning. It'll send the same message. Fischer, go upstairs and find Voigt. Tell him to get the men who are going to deliver the bombs to the divers' sheds. And alert the divers."

Regaining his composure and confidence, Schwegel returned to the laboratory and wrote out a revised schedule, moving everything forward one day.

⸻❖⸻

Through the remainder of the afternoon, as last checks were done of each bomb case, Voigt brought men downstairs to get final instructions and to pick up the bombs. They would meet with their divers at three boat sheds rented over the last month on the New Jersey side of the Hudson, on the East River, and at the foot of 74th Street in Manhattan on the Hudson. Used but seaworthy launches had been bought and stored in the sheds. At about midnight, the three boats, with two divers and two armed guards in each, would be launched to make their stealthy approaches to the target ships.

"Vat's left?" Voigt asked, as the last of the East River bombs went out the laboratory door.

Schwegel read the tags. On the table were four bombs still to be checked, but they were in shoeboxes. "Rockefeller, Astor, the police headquarters, and City Hall."

"I have da men for doze upstairs. Should I bring dem down togeder or one at a time? Dey'll need special instructions"

Schwegel glanced at his watch. "No. I want to eat my dinner first."

"Don't you tink we should get dem out first?"

"If I thought we should get them out first, Herr Voigt, I would have said so. Come back in an hour."

"But sir, can't —"

Schwegel's sharp glare ended the conversation. Voigt retreated through the laboratory door which Schwegel locked behind him.

From the ice chest, he drew a wrapped plate of bratwurst, a tin of asparagus, and two pears wrapped in newspaper. From another chest, he took out a bottle of Niersteiner wine.

Laying the food, a linen napkin, and silverware on the laboratory table next to the Rockefeller bomb, he prepared to eat, but then rose to do one more thing.

On the gramophone, he placed a record, a recording of Wagner's *Das Rheingold*, and cranked the instrument a dozen times.

Then he took the first bites of the bratwurst and closed his eyes to savor the food as well as the strains of Wagner that quietly began to fill the laboratory.

How strange, he thought, that one could find moments of such bliss in the middle of a war.

Herr Voigt sits in the dark

40

Escape

NOLAN COUNTED SEVEN bullet holes in the closet door, a thin ray of light shining through each. Because of the pallets and garbage cans that blocked the door from the outside, he was able to see clearly through only one. He could spot the feet of the guard as he paced the outer room.

One bullet left. It had to count.

Now he heard the metal door between the outer room and the machinery room open, bringing in the din of the machines.

"Gunther, stay awake."

Nolan recognized the voice of the second German.

"I'm trying."

"How's our friend?"

"I been putting a new bullet in da door every fifteen minutes."

"Maybe it's time for a few more."

Nolan crept back to his protected corner. Three bullets

exploded through the door, then a long silence followed.

"Maybe we got him," the second German said.

More silence.

"We could check."

Nolan kicked a garbage can. "I wouldn't, if I were you."

"I'll be back later," the second German called out. "And you won't survive when I do come back, I promise you."

Again, Nolan heard the machine room door open and shut. Cautiously, he moved out of his corner to his door to examine the holes. He squinted through two of the new ones, but they were both partially blocked by pallets. Then he noticed that the third new hole near the floor, just beyond the pallets but in their shadow, had enlarged a previous one. In the dark, he felt around the room for a makeshift tool, finding a piece of a metal bar in the trash can. The end fit snugly through the enlarged hole, and with the noise from the machine room drowning out what he was doing, he slowly worked the bar back and forth to enlarge it further, splintering off pieces of the wood periodically. After a few minutes, the hole was as large as his fist. A second hole a foot above it allowed him to lie on the floor, point his revolver through the large hole, and see where he was aiming through the higher hole, although he knew the aim would be questionable.

He had to wait nearly five minutes for a promising moment to arrive. The guard started pacing again, perhaps to drive off sleep. At first, his gait was relatively fast and a shot had as much chance of hitting as missing. Then Nolan saw him reach into his pocket for his pipe and a match. He knew the guard would stop to light it.

The question was where he would be when he did.

However, the guard stopped out of sight. Despite the noise of the machines, Nolan heard the match strike, then the pacing began again. The pipe must not have been sufficiently lit, though, because the guard stopped to light another match. This time, he was within sight.

Nolan aimed at the center of his chest and fired. The guard dropped to the floor instantly. The body was motionless, but Nolan could not see where the shot had hit because of the pallets. He stood to see through a hole higher in the door that was not blocked. A pool of blood was rapidly forming under the man's head, not his chest. The blood was running from his eye. A lucky shot.

Nolan tried pushing the door open but could barely budge the weight in front of it. He realized he was weak after so many hours without food. He also realized the second German would soon be back.

Suddenly, the noise of the machinery in the building stopped. The factory must have shut down, Nolan thought, whether for Good Friday or for the need to move the bombs out of the building without the workers seeing it.

Mustering all his strength, he leaned his shoulder into the door and shoved. This time, it moved but barely two inches. Another shove, two more inches. A last shove and the door was open enough that he could squeeze out.

He grabbed the guard's pistol and took a handful of bullets from his pocket. He saw they were thirty-eight caliber and would fit his Smith & Wesson revolver, so he tossed the pistol. Then he cracked open the alley door. No good. There were automobiles parked in the alley and men around them, likely Germans. As he slowly closed it, he realized it was night. He had completely lost track of the time. Was it nearing midnight? Were they going to be too late?

Next he tried the machinery room door, opening it just an inch. The lights were off. The room was lit only by the street light coming through the high, barred windows. It appeared empty, so Nolan began to cautiously cross the cement floor to the entryway to 38th Street.

Startling him, Nolan saw a figure sitting motionless by a workbench ten feet from him. Instinctively, he reached for his revolver just as the figure turned toward him.

"You're Becker's man, aren't you? Sweeney?"

"Uh, yes. Herr Voigt?"

"Yes. I've had a man out looking for you all day. I guess he found you. Da plans have changed. Ve might need you tonight after all."

Nolan, thinking about the second German, kept his hand on his revolver. "That's what I was told … that the plans changed. But I wasn't told exactly how."

"Everyting has been moved up a day. The police vere here dis morning. Dey're starting to figure it out, so da bombs will be put in place tonight to go off tomorrow. It von't make no difference vetter it's Easter Sunday or Holy Saturday. Da message vill be da same."

"I see."

"But right now, da chemist is downstairs eating, so da vorld has come to a stop vile he eats his fool dinner. I vould suggest you go find yourself a spot to sit down and have a pipe for about tirty minutes. Ven he finishes, den ve'll need you."

"Need me for what?"

"Da bombs for da ships in da harbor vent out about

an hour ago. Dey'll all be placed on da hulls after midnight. But dere are still bombs to be set on some buildings. An interesting list. Da homes of da Astors and da Rockefellers and such places."

"Placed when? And you don't know the time right now, do you?"

"Doze bombs vill be set after midnight also. I believe it's about seven-tirty right now. Go have your pipe. And if you hear vat sounds like gunshots in da building, don't vorry. Ve have a policeman trapped in a storage room. Ignore dem."

"Thirty minutes. I'll be ready," Nolan said.

Nolan, trying to appear as casual as possible, ambled away. His first thought was to find an unguarded exit door and escape the building. The danger was too great. He would find a public phone and try to call Tunney to tell him of the change in plan, then it would be up to Tunney to stop the plot.

However, as he walked away, he considered the danger to the city of New York, to its residents. Could he live with himself if he ran at this crucial moment if there was something else he could have done by staying in the building? And now that he had sufficient bullets and his revolver back and the element of surprise − Voigt thinking he was one of them − might he be relatively safe in the midst of the danger?

Now he saw there were offices at the far end of the machinery room. When he was convinced Voigt could no longer see him, he ducked into the shipping manager's office and closed the door. There was a telephone on the desk, so he got on the floor behind the desk, taking the instrument with him. He had memorized Tunney's office number and the central operator passed him through quickly.

"What?"

"Sir, this is John."

"Why are you whispering?"

"I have to."

Nolan explained the change in the situation. The bombs were to be set that night to go off at noon tomorrow, Satuday. The targets were mainly ships in the harbor and the bombs would be attached to their hulls. The divers were getting ready in boat sheds now. "They'll start placing all the bombs at midnight. But they'll also be going after the homes of Rockefeller and Astor."

"We already have police around the harbor and we have our own divers with them," Tunney said. "We'll catch them."

Then Nolan explained where he was and that he intended to try to get downstairs to the bomb laboratory.

"I'll alert the harbor police and my detectives then we'll come find you," Tunney said. "Good luck."

The foreman guards the laboratory

41

The Hidden Door

AS HE MOVED back across the machinery room, Nolan could vaguely see Voigt sitting in the same place. A dozen steps beyond him was the metal door to the basement.

Voigt turned as he approached.

"Are we ready yet, sir?" Nolan asked as he put his hand on his revolver.

"No. I tell you ven. Go back to your pipe."

"Would you like me to check with the man in the basement?" he asked Voigt.

"Da chemist? No. Leave him alone."

"Maybe his dinner is done and he expects us down there."

Frowning, Voigt looked up at him. "If I vanted you to check on him, I'd of told you to check on him. Vouldn't I?"

"Yes, sir. Sorry."

"I sent a man down dere to guard him and to inform

us when he's ready. Just go sit someplace and vait."

Nolan moved behind nearby machinery and raised the revolver to shoot Voigt, but there was a sudden commotion in the storage room which Voigt immediately rose to investigate, vanishing into the room's darkness. Nolan guessed the dead German had finally been discovered. Knowing what would quickly follow, Nolan crept to the basement door. This would be his best chance to get the Easter man.

Once Voigt was across the room, Nolan opened it. The huge foreman, who had tried to stop him from going down earlier in the day, was standing at the bottom of the steps, a rifle at his side. Seeing Nolan, he began to raise the rifle, but Nolan had his revolver ready and fired twice, dropping the man in a heap to the brick floor. Then Nolan quickly closed the metal door behind himself and bolted it from the inside.

It did not take him long to find the hidden door to the laboratory, but it was locked.

"What's going on out there?" The voice came from inside. The chemist. The Easter man.

Then pounding started on the door at the top of the stairs.

"Some trouble," Nolan said. "I've been sent down here to guard you."

There was silence from inside the hidden laboratory, then silence from upstairs. Nolan realized he could be seen from the basement windows, so he unscrewed the overhead light bulb and got behind the furnace in the dark.

"Has it stopped?" The chemist asked.

"I can't tell," Nolan said. "Do you need me in there?"

"Who are you?"

"Sweeney. One of Voigt's men."

More silence. Nolan thought of the blacked-out windows on the laboratory side of the basement. The Germans might try to warn the chemist through them.

"Sir, there may be police in the alley. You should stay away from the windows and come out here. Herr Voigt has a motor ready for you and men to guard you."

The laboratory door did not open. If the Germans did convince him to open the basement windows, the chemist might be able to pass the remaining bombs up to them, but the windows were too small for him to escape through. The Easter man was trapped.

Nolan heard voices in the alley and went to the laboratory door. Pressing an ear to it, he heard the chemist answering the voices in whispers.

The silence returned but was soon broken by the window glass on Nolan's side of the basement shattering. He rushed behind the furnace just as bullets began flying into the room, ricocheting off the brick wall. One punctured the furnace, sending a hiss of steam into the air by his face, before the firing ended.

"Are you still out there?" It was the chemist.

"I'm not going anywhere," Nolan said.

"I know you're the police. And I don't care. You won't stop what we're doing."

"Your bombs in the harbor? We already have men out there to catch your divers. Not a single ship will be lost."

"I doubt that. But you know, I'm in the German military. This is war. All your judges will do is intern me for a few years then deport me when the fighting is done. If you read your newspapers, you know your judges treat combatants differently."

"Then come out and give yourself up."

Nolan got no response, giving him time to think. Was it true? Would the courts just give him a mild punishment then send him back to Germany as if war were a fair thing, fought with gentlemen's rules, no matter how horrible the crime?

"You know," the chemist eventually said. "If I wanted, I could blow up this entire building, with all the TNT I have in here."

"Go ahead," Nolan said. "But you'd die in an instant."

"So would you, though. I might enjoy that, knowing you died too."

"When would you enjoy that exactly, if you're dead?"

"It's the anticipation of it. Your head exploding from the pressure, the heat melting your eyes. I would think about it before I lit the fuse. It would give me pleasure.'

"It would explode your head and melt your eyes too. You should think about that."

"Then again, I might not even bother to blow you up. I'll just serve my punishment then go back to Germany and live a long happy life and I'll let you die a natural death in your bed. Isn't that kind of me?"

The silence between them returned. A standoff. Then another round of bullets was fired into his side of the basement, with at least two revolvers shooting this time, and it did not stop. Nolan had to fold himself into an even smaller target behind the furnace as he waited out the relentless barrage.

The Easter man

42

The Final Threat

THERE HAD BEEN no sound from the alley or from inside the laboratory for nearly twenty minutes when the commotion started upstairs in the machinery room.

Nolan crept to the top of the stairs to listen, peering through the crack between the bottom of the door and the floor. When he saw a New York City police uniform, he pounded on the door.

"Police! Down here! Is Tunney out there?"

"John, is that you?" It was Tunney's voice.

"Yes, sir. Their bombmaker is trapped down here. But he still has TNT. He threatened to blow up the building. You better get out."

Then Nolan heard the laboratory door creaking open behind him. "Don't bother. I'm coming out and there's no bomb."

His revolver in hand, Nolan rushed down the stairs and screwed back in the overhead light. The chemist, lighting a pipe and looking unworried, stood in the doorway.

So this was him. The Easter man.

Dressed in a well pressed suit, perhaps thirty, with a slim frame, beard, and thinning hair, he appeared like a university professor. He looked too bookish, too harmless, to be the man behind such a plan of havoc.

Keeping his revolver trained on him, Nolan directed him up the stairs to where Tunney and other detectives waited in the machinery room.

Tunney put the handcuffs on him. "You're done, my friend. We have our own divers in the river right now and they've already found many of your magnet bombs. I promise you we'll get the rest before tomorrow. So you're headed to prison."

"This doesn't concern me," the Easter man said. "I'll be on my way back to Germany in two or three years. This is about war."

"There's more. One of your comrades, who's got a wife and child to protect, told us it was your bomb that took down the ferry last week."

"It won't matter. This has all been about war. It isn't personal."

Tunney spun him around to look into his face. "You admit you sank that ferry?"

"I don't admit anything."

"More than fifty people died."

"If they did, they were casualties of the war ... assuming the ferry was part of this, and I'm not saying it was. Judges would not treat combatants the same as others in their court. So I'm not worried."

"You tell me what war materials that ferry was carrying? It was ferrying people, innocent people, to and from their jobs. No judge will see it as part of any war. That's murder, fifty counts of murder. And for that, you'll never see the outside of one of our fine prisons again and you'll be lucky if the electric chair isn't your fate."

"You have no proof I had anything to do with that sinking besides what some desperate fool told you to save himself."

Tunney broke into a broad smile. "But my friend, we may very well have proof."

"I seriously doubt that," Schwegel said with a smile just as broad.

Challenged, Tunney leaned in close and whispered. "Your comrade told us more about the ferry. The second bomb you put out that night? On *The India Light*? The bomb that wasn't meant to explode? That ship still hasn't left the harbor. Its engine is under repair. Right now, my divers are going over it and I'll bet they'll find the bomb casing still stuck to the hull with magnets. And I'll bet it'll be identical to the other casings we're recovering tonight."

The Easter man's stone-faced confidence finally faded. He saw Tunney's victorious expression and his own expression hardened. As he passed Nolan while being led away, he spit at him, something Nolan easily side-stepped.

Tunney threw an arm around Nolan. "John, great work. This city owes you all the gratitude in the world. We'll get every one of these bastards. We've already caught or killed most of them. Our men will be holding up the ships in the harbor until they can all be examined."

Through a window onto the alley, Nolan saw Hauxthausen being handcuffed and placed in a police motor van. Nolan pointed him out to Tunney, telling him he was the one who attacked the officer on Pelham Parkway.

"The bastard. He won't be getting bail any time soon," Tunney said.

In the front hallway, a dozen policemen were assembling everyone caught in the building, putting handcuffs and leg shackles on them. One of the cuffed men was Paul O'Keefe who turned sharply when Nolan passed.

"I heard what you did and I know your real name, you dog," he said. "It's O'Connell. Even in prison, I'll get word to our people. We'll find you O'Connell, then what will your life be worth?"

Nolan kept walking, smiling to himself.

Outside, on the sidewalk, as more shackled men were led to the rear of the van, Tunney took Nolan aside again to speak to him in confidence.

"This will be in all the newspapers tomorrow, John. But your name won't be mentioned. One more thing. Your address – is it still that Clinton Avenue apartment in Brooklyn?"

"Yes, sir."

"J. P. Morgan was told we prevented the assassination attempt on him, so his man found me a few minutes ago. Morgan wants to send me a reward check, a thousand dollars. Cheap son of a bitch that he thinks that's all saving his life is worth. But I can't take a reward. I'm a city official. You aren't, though. I'll have his man send the check to you instead. You earned it, John. Just don't mention it to anyone."

Tunney shook Nolan's hand a last time then went to accompany the van downtown. Nolan surveyed the scene for a moment, feeling a pride at his part in it but also an accumulated exhaustion now that it was over.

Turning, he began to walk the ten blocks to his apartment on West 49th Street. However, he got only a few steps when he realized he never had to spend a night there again. With that, he felt a wave of relief then a jolt of excitement as he spotted a trolley going west.

The emotions rising in him, he began to run to catch it, calculating the trip as he did. The trolley to the subway at Broadway, then south to City Hall, then the elevated over to Brooklyn.

Brooklyn and Sheenagh and home.

– END –

About the author

Stan Freeman is a former journalist whose articles have appeared in more than two dozen newspapers, including the *San Francisco Chronicle*, *Seattle Times*, *New Orleans Times-Picayune*, *Houston Chronicle* and *St. Louis Post-Dispatch*. He spent much of his career as the science and environmental writer for the *Springfield Union-News* and *Sunday Republican* of Massachusetts.

Born in New York City, he studied engineering at Cornell University and fiction writing in the MFA program at University of Massachusetts. He's published several short stories in literary magazines and has held a fiction-writing fellowship from the Massachusetts Council on the Arts and Humanities.

His historical mystery, *The Dutton Girl*, was released by the Seattle-based publisher, Coffeetown Press, in June of 2018.

He lives in western Massachusetts.